STREET HAWK 3: GOLDEN EYES

Street Hawk was a motorcycle, but it was unlike any motorcycle Jesse had ever ridden before. Its speed was incredible; in the computer-assisted hyperthrust mode, Jesse had clocked speeds of well over three hundred miles per hour. It was equipped with a vertical lift system that could fire the motorcycle up to thirty metres into the air, enabling it to sail over obstacles that would stop any other vehicle. The motorcycle had a number of highly developed attack and defence systems and it was hooked up to a computer that constantly monitored it for any technical malfunction.

These were all reasons why Jesse loved riding Street Hawk. But the most important reason of all was the way the bike handled whenever he rode it. There were times it felt almost like an extension of his own body, and Jesse's moves had become so instinctive that he often felt the motorcycle was responding to his thoughts before he was consciously aware of them himself. . .

HAPPY

BIRTHDAY

TO CHORDA —

From

DABHAI

D1173380

STREET HAWK 3: GOLDEN EYES

A novel by Charles Gale

Based on the Universal television series 'Street Hawk'
Created by Robert Wolterstorff & Paul M. Belous
and Bruce Lansbury
Adapted from the episodes 'Follow the Yellow Gold Road'
written by Burton Armus, and 'Dog Eat Dog',
written by Nicholas Corea and Bruce Cervi

TARGET

A TARGET BOOK

published by
the Paperback Division of
W.H. ALLEN & Co. PLC

A Target Book
Published in 1985
by the Paperback Division of
W.H. Allen & Co. PLC
44 Hill Street, London W1X 8LB

Phototypeset by Hart Typesetting Services, Basingstoke, Hants.
Printed and bound in Great Britain by
Anchor Brendon Ltd, Tiptree, Essex

ISBN 0 426 20191 4

ONE

The white Mustang sped down the highway as the hot noon sun burned brightly overhead. Jesse Mach was singing along with the song playing on his tapedeck, at the top of his lungs—and as if he didn't have a care in the world. He glanced down at the speedometer and seeing that he was doing just over sixty miles per hour, eased up on the accelerator a bit, bringing his speed down to a legal fifty-five. If a 'black and white' clocked him going over the speed limit, he had no doubt they would pull him over and give him a ticket, just for the fun of it. Not that Jesse would have any right to complain; when he was a motorcycle cop, he had probably given speeding tickets to half the guys on the force. And turnabout, as he'd been reminded three days ago when he got his last ticket, was fair play.

Jesse's mind had wandered from his speed because he was too wrapped up in the music blaring out of his stereo speakers. He loved that song. He loved that voice. *'He's got golden eyes . . . he's got a silver tongue . . .'* Jesse sang along with the chorus. The singer was Deborah Shain, the new uncrowned queen of rock and roll. She was the latest overnight sensation in a business known for overnight sensations. Six months ago, no one had even heard of her. And now, she'd had three hit singles and an album that had been riding the top of the charts for months. The woman was, in the vernacular of the rock world, totally hot.

Jesse was on his way to meet Deborah Shain. It was far and away the most pleasant task he'd had to perform since he had started working for the Police Department's Public Relations office. Usually, his days were filled with exciting activities like giving department tours to school children, setting up the Neighbourhood Watch Programme, and writing press releases and anti-litter pamphlets. Meanwhile, his new co-worker in the office, Rachel Adams, was meeting rock stars and movie stars, shooting television commercials, and hobnobbing with the rich and powerful. It was all a result of the anti-drug spots the department was filming. It was Rachel's pet project, and she had no intention of letting Jesse get anywhere near it.

Rachel had been the one who initially came up with the idea of trying to get Deborah Shain to do one of the spots. Jesse kindly volunteered to talk to Deborah for her, since Rachel seemed to be buried under all her other work, but Rachel wasn't buying it. 'The anti-drug campaign is my baby,' she said haughtily. 'You have your own work to do.'

So Rachel tried to get in touch with Deborah Shain. And failed miserably. Her manager refused to let Rachel talk to her. He said she wasn't interested, she didn't do favours for the police department, and Rachel should leave her alone. Rachel was persistent and continued to call, almost daily, until Deborah's manager learned to recognize her voice and began hanging up on her before Rachel could even get a sentence out.

That's when Rachel came to Jesse, asking if perhaps he could apply some of his much-vaunted charm to the situation. Maybe he, Rachel suggested, could succeed where she had failed. Jesse was too clever to jump at the opportunity the way he would have several days before. He intended to make Rachel pay for hogging all the glamorous work the department had to offer, leaving him only the scraps. He played it cool, claiming he had much too much other work to do to take time out of his busy schedule to talk to some rock and roll singer. Rachel begged, Rachel pleaded, Rachel cajoled, and finally, Jesse relented, agreeing to do this one favour for her. So now, not only did Jesse have an excuse to meet one of his favourite singers in the whole world, but he had the additional satisfaction of having Rachel in his debt for offering him a task he would have cut off his left ear to have.

This was the first time he could remember actually looking forward to doing something for Public Relations. When he'd first been placed in PR, after the accident that had ended his career as a motorcycle cop, he had actually considered quitting the police department, despite the fact he used to think such a day would never come. All his life, it seemed, the only thing he had ever really wanted to be was a police officer. Even when he became a big star on the motorcycle circuit, winning the AMA Grand National three years running and garnering a dozen medals in the International Six Day Trials, he never forgot that this was just a temporary diversion before he embarked on his real career as a policeman. When he finally joined the force and found himself cruising the streets of the city and speeding off to rescue helpless crime victims, like a modern-day Sir Lancelot, he felt utterly and totally fulfilled. He couldn't imagine ever wanting to do anything else with his life. So when the department informed him that the knee injury he'd received in his accident precluded his ever being able to ride a motorcycle again, Jesse felt like his life was over.

That's when Norman Tuttle came along. Norman offered Jesse a chance to ride again. There was a new kind of prosthetic device that had just been developed. Norman told Jesse he could arrange an operation for him. The procedure had not yet received Government approval, but Norman had powerful connections in the government and he could persuade the FDA to turn a blind eye to this breach of regulations. All Jesse had to do was agree to his terms. Jesse agreed; he would do whatever was necessary to be able to ride again. So, Jesse's knee was repaired and in return, he became an employee of the Federal Government, testing a new piece of machinery that Norman had spent the past four years of his life developing.

Street Hawk.

Street Hawk was a motorcyle, but it was unlike any motorcycle Jesse had ever ridden before. Its speed was incredible; in the computer-assisted hyperthrust mode, Jesse had clocked speeds of well over three hundred miles per hour. It was equipped with a vertical lift system that could fire the motorcycle up to thirty metres into the air, enabling it to sail over obstacles that would stop any other vehicle. The motorcycle had a number of highly developed attack and defence systems and it was hooked up to a computer that constantly monitored it for any technical malfunction, as well as surveying the surrounding area for any possible danger. In addition, every time he went out, Norman watched Jesse's progress on closed-circuit video. It was like having an extra pair of eyes.

These were all reasons why Jesse loved riding Street Hawk. But as far as he was concerned, the most important reason of all was the way the bike handled whenever he rode it. It simply responded better than any motorcycle Jesse had ever tested. There were times it felt almost like an extension of his own body, and Jesse's moves had become so instinctive that he often felt the motorcycle was responding to his thoughts before he was consciously aware of them himself.

Street Hawk was, for the present at least, an undercover operation. The Government was afraid the public would not appreciate having a technologically sophisticated attack motorcycle, hooked up by computer to information systems all over the city, patrolling the streets. So although Street Hawk was a constant subject of newspaper articles, no one knew of the Government's involvement. Nor did anyone know of Jesse's involvement. When he donned his racing suit and helmet, he also donned a second identity, that of Street Hawk, the vigilante crime-fighter. That was why Jesse had to continue his work in Police Department Public Relations. He could allow no one to suspect who he really was. Because the Police Department was trying to capture Street Hawk and put him out of business, claiming the city had no use for a self-styled vigilante, Jesse often felt he was straddling both sides of the fence, condemning by day the activities he performed at night. He felt like he was two separate people. And considering the ridiculous activities the department sometimes required of him, he wasn't sure he didn't like Street Hawk better.

Jesse was almost at Silver Screen Studios by now. He took the next exit and drove through the few blocks of residential streets that remained between him and his destination. He was still singing along to the Deborah Shain song playing on his tapedeck, when he stopped at a red light. The two teenage girls in the blue convertible next to him watched him singing and started to giggle. He looked out the window and flashed the girls his most winning smile.

The blonde with braces in the passenger seat leaned over and whispered, 'He's cute,' to the dark-haired driver. The whisper was just loud enough for Jesse to hear, and both girls smiled back at him. The light changed and Jesse turned right at the corner, leaving the girls behind as just a memory.

Jesse's smile won them over every time. It melted hearts the way a hot Sahara sun melted ice cream cones. Jesse didn't think he was particularly vain, but he knew he was good-looking. He always had plenty of girls around to assure him of that fact, and new conquests came easily to him. Tall, slim, with brown wavy hair, he had the kind of boyish face that assured women he knew how to handle himself but could be as gentle as the proverbial lamb in the right circumstances. He didn't think he'd have any trouble charming Deborah Shain.

There was a security guard at the studio gate when Jesse arrived. While the guard was looking him over, Jesse pulled out his badge, showed it to him, and, trying to sound as official as possible, asked where he might find Deborah Shain.

'They're shooting over on Stage Six,' the guard explained, and gave him instructions on how to find it. Jesse thanked him and started across the lot. From the amount of activity Jesse could see as he drove past the sound stages, it appeared the studio was very busy. Trucks drove by carrying scenery, shuttle buses ran busy executives from one end of the lot to the other, and all along the road, technicians were engaged in purposeful conversations, totally oblivious to the traffic around them. It was Jesse's understanding that music videos were the major source of income here now, although in years gone by a number of well-known motion pictures had been shot on Silver Screen's backlot. It was said that there still remained a number of exterior sets on the backlot here; since the space was not needed, no one had ever bothered to dismantle them, and it was felt that as long as the sets remained in place, it was possible someone might find another use for them. In fact, Jesse seemed to recall having seen a music video shot on a Western street on Silver Screen's backlot. He couldn't remember the song, but he remembered being impressed by the set.

Jesse found Stage Six and parked his car on the side of the road. There was a Winnebago trailer parked nearby, with the name of Deborah's record label, R-Jay Records, emblazoned across it. If Jesse wanted to go through proper channels, it would be best for him to knock on the door of the motor home and ask permission before he barged on stage and tried to see Deborah. But Jesse had never been the type to do things through proper channels. Besides, as long as he didn't ask permission, no one could say no.

There was a guard standing outside the sound stage, but all Jesse had to do was flash him his badge and explain that he was on official business, and the guard granted him immediate access. Jesse stepped inside and looked around. He was quite impressed. A surrealistic street scene had been constructed inside the mammoth building. There were huge storefronts, painted in bright garish shades of green and orange, and flashing neon signs hung above the backdrops, advertising their names in a language unlike any on Earth. The street itself was a grid of lights, constantly changing colours and flashing geometric shapes. At the far end of the street, the set changed from ultra-modern to post-apocalyptical, with shattered windows and cinder blocks and steel girders littered all along the street.

The members of the cast were standing around waiting for another take. They were dressed in leather and chains and their skins were painted white. One man with a purple

10

Mohawk held two German Shepherds, also decked out in leather, on a leash. All the actors carried some kind of weapon, a gun or a knife or a tomahawk.

The only man standing in front of the camera who looked normal was a bearded blond man whom Jesse immediately assumed was the director. He was talking quietly with a young lady dressed in a skin-tight silver body suit that covered her completely from the neck down. She had black horizontal lines painted across her stark white face, and diamond-shaped figures around her eyes. She looked like a refugee from a nightmare, but even decked out like this, she radiated a certain presence. Deborah Shain was recognizable no matter how she was dressed.

'All right, let's try it again,' the director said, speaking with a British accent. 'Places, everyone.' He clapped his hands together and the actors quickly moved to their positions. Deborah walked to a spot about halfway down the street and the rest of the cast lined up some twenty yards behind her. The director walked over to his seat beside the camera and regarded the set, stroking his beard thoughtfully. 'Roll them,' he said.

The camera started running and a woman stepped in front of the set, announced the scene and take number and clapped a slate. She stepped away and the director shouted out, 'Start playback!' The sound man switched on a tape player and a moment later, a Deborah Shain song came blasting over the speaker system. Deborah lip-synced the words, moving down the street in a stylized half-run, half-dance, darting anxious glances behind her like a damsel in distress. The other members of the cast, weapons aloft, chased her down the street, the dogs in the lead. The camera was mounted on a track and it rolled forward, keeping pace with Deborah's movements.

Deborah stopped at the door of one of the storefronts and opened it, and a skeleton flew out at her, cued by a fancy guitar riff on the tape. Deborah screamed in mock terror and continued to run, the others in hot pursuit. She reached the bombed-out end of the street and ducked inside one of the crumbling buildings, tripping over the rubble as she tried to hide from her pursuers. The other members of the cast followed her as she disappeared behind a partially-demolished brick wall. The director waited until the last of them slipped from sight and then yelled, 'That's it! Cut!'

The camera stopped, the sound man switched off the music, and the actors climbed out from behind the set, dropping their poses as deadly assassins. The last one out was Deborah. She approached the director and said, 'Well, how was it?'

'Downright silly, love,' he answered. Deborah frowned and, seeing her look, he put his hand on her shoulder to reassure her. 'Oh no, not you. My staging. It looks like a bloody cartoon. We're not going to be giving the little tykes nightmares with this one.'

Deborah laughed. 'I didn't know we were trying to give anyone nightmares. I thought we were trying to sell records.'

'If they can't sleep, they'll buy the records,' the director assured her. He moved toward the set, scratching his beard and mumbling to himself, 'Maybe it's the dogs. They don't seem to have the right rhythm.'

The assistant director approached him and the two men exchanged a couple of words. The director nodded and his assistant shouted to the waiting members of the crew, 'This might be a while. Why don't we break for lunch?'

There was a scattering of applause as people started to move toward the door. The make-up lady, a thin wan brunette with sharp elbows, hurried over to Deborah with two damp towels.

Jesse waited patiently while the members of the cast and crew walked out the door past him. He wanted to catch Deborah alone, when she wouldn't have too many distractions. In a moment, the only people remaining were the director, who was walking through the set making suggestions to his assistant, and Deborah, who was wiping the heavy paint off her face with the aid of the make-up lady.

Jesse moved toward her. She had her back to him and he hesitated a moment, almost afraid to speak. For a brief second, he didn't feel like a police officer at all; he just felt like another fan, asking a big star for her autograph. He cleared his throat.

'Uh, Miss Shain . . .?'

She turned around. Jesse felt his heart stop, and for an instant, the thought passed through his head that were he to die then and there, it would be as a happy man. He had seen pictures, of course, but they hadn't done her justice. She was gorgeous. Wearing the incongruous make-up, Deborah had looked tough and resilient, but now she looked just the opposite, all sweetness and innocence, almost angelic. Blonde and blue-eyed, she had soft round features and clear unblemished skin; a face that reminded him of open country fields and cool moonlit nights.

He stared at her, and she stared back. Jesse felt almost overcome by the urge to wrap his arms around her and hold her and kiss her. And from the look in her eyes, he felt she would respond in kind, never worrying about the fact that they hadn't spoken and she didn't even know his name. But the feeling passed, replaced by an acute embarrassment over how silly they must both look, staring at each other like two schoolkids in the first awakenings of adolescence.

'My name's Jesse Mach,' he said, recalling them both to reality. 'I'm with the Police Department.'

The angelic look on her face disappeared, and in its stead appeared a range of expressions, first curiosity, then fear, then anger. She shot a look at her make-up lady, then gave Jesse a cold stare and said savagely, 'What do you want with me, cop?'

Jesse held up his hands, trying to calm her down. 'Hey, no need to get excited. I just wanted to talk to you about doing a public service announcement for us.'

Deborah turned away, looking in the mirror the make-up lady held up for her. 'Didn't you already talk to my manager about this?'

'Yes, but—'

'And he said I wasn't interested,' Deborah finished. She wiped away the few remaining traces of make-up around her eyes. 'He was right. I'm not interested.'

'Your manager didn't even want to hear what these public

service announcements were for,' Jesse explained.

'I'm sure it's for a very worthy cause,' Deborah said sarcastically, 'and if it's a donation you want, I'll write you a big fat cheque.'

'We don't need your money. It's your time we want.'

'I said I'm not interested!' Deborah repeated, handing the towel back. 'Thanks, Jackie,' she said.

'You know, a public service announcement from you could really help some kids out there having problems.'

Deborah hesitated. Jesse, seeing his opening, pressed the attack. 'You see, we're trying to combat drug use among teenagers. A lot of people in the entertainment industry make drugs look very exciting and glamorous and that's what gets some of these kids started in the first place; they want to imitate their idols. We want to counter that impression by putting TV spots on the air that show big stars like you and others warning kids about the dangers of drugs. Maybe it will take some of the glamour away from it.'

Deborah looked at him, still hesitant. She bit her lip and looked away. 'I'm sorry. I'm sure you mean well, and I don't want to be nasty about this, but I can't. I just can't.'

'If you convinced one kid not to experiment with drugs, don't you think it would be worth your time?' From the way she stood there, not moving, Jesse could tell she was considering it, but then she moved toward the door. Jesse called after her, 'You know, a lot of kids really look up to you—'

Deborah stepped out into the sunlight without looking back.

Jesse turned to the make-up lady with a confused look on his face. 'What is it? Is it me?'

The woman shook her head. 'No. She just has this thing about cops.'

Jesse raised his eyebrows. 'Thanks,' he said. He hurried out the door after her.

Deborah was standing in line at the catering truck parked next to the stage. There were picnic tables all around and the oddly-dressed members of the cast were sitting at them, having lunch. Jesse got in line behind her. She pretended to ignore him while she chose herself a salad, but Jesse was not so

14

easily put off.

'So, what have you got against cops?' he asked.

Deborah shot him a dirty look. 'Jackie's got a big mouth,' she said. 'Look, everybody's got their thing. There're plenty of big stars whose thing is doing public service commercials. Can't you get someone else?'

'Sure, we can get someone else. But then, they wouldn't be Deborah Shain, would they? You know, the kids of this country have been real good for you and your career. Maybe it's time you did something for them.'

She moved away from him and sat down at one of the picnic tables, all by herself. Jesse grabbed a handful of carrots off the catering truck and sat down at the table across from her. He gazed at her, trying to attract her attention, but she picked at her salad and refused to look up.

He took a huge chomp out of his carrot stick and leaned over toward her, saying in his best Bugs Bunny impersonation, 'So, what's up, doc?'

Deborah smiled despite herself. She looked up at Jesse and he showed her his perfect row of white teeth in an ingratiating grin.

'You know, you're not like most other policemen I've met,' Deborah admitted.

'I hope that's a compliment,' Jesse said.

Her smile broadened. 'It is.'

'So, why don't you let me take you out to dinner and try to talk you into doing this promo?' Jesse suggested.

Deborah gave him a look and shook her head. 'Sorry. No way.'

'Which? The talk or the date?'

'Both, I'm afraid.'

'Hey, what's wrong?' Jesse said, holding out his arms as if exhibiting himself. 'I'm kind, I'm charming, I'm gallant, and I know this little Japanese restaurant.'

Deborah continued to shake her head. 'I'm sorry, it's just impossible. I've got a—' she groped for the right word '—friend.'

'Oh.' Jesse looked disappointed. 'Is it serious?'

Deborah turned back to her salad. 'No,' she said, and

Jesse could hear the strain in her voice. 'It was, once, but that's all over now. Right now it's just a mess. I'm trying to break it off, but, I don't know, it just doesn't make any sense. Anyway, going out with somebody else wouldn't help matters.'

Jesse could tell Deborah was upset, a lot more upset than she wanted anyone to realize. 'You want to talk about it?' he asked, concerned.

She shook her head. 'I'm sorry, I can't.'

'You sure?'

'I'm sure,' she answered. 'I don't want to talk about him.'

TWO

At that moment, the man Deborah Shain didn't want to talk about was less than a hundred yards away, inside the motor home Jesse had noticed when he'd first arrived. The man's name was Virgil Powell and he was Deborah's manager. Powell was a tall thin man with short red hair and a nasty-looking scar across his left cheek. The other man in the room was Neil Jacobs, the President of R-Jay Records. Jacobs was smaller than Powell, and heavier. He'd recently had a hair transplant which hadn't taken very well. His head was covered with small plugs of hair, giving it the appearance of an imperfectly mown lawn.

Jacobs was the kind of man who favoured the ostentatious in everything. He wore only the latest styles and cared more about the name on the label than he did about the colour or the fabric. He loved jewellery and usually wore two or three gold chains around his neck. He was rarely seen in public without his favourite gold bracelet, garnished with a setting of brilliant diamonds, adorning his wrist. His taste was further reflected by the furnishings inside the Winnebago. Although he rarely used the place as an office, he insisted on decorating it with the most fashionable of high-tech furniture, all silver and glass. Several pieces of modern art hung on the walls. He kept a complete home entertainment set-up there—a stereo system, a compact disc player, and several different brands of VCRs, even though these technological wonders were rarely, if ever, used. He also kept a fully-stocked bar that was used all the time.

Jacobs was standing at it now, pouring himself a glass of Scotch. 'Can I offer you something, Virgil?' Jacobs asked.

'I didn't come here to drink,' Powell said, pacing back and forth behind Jacobs. 'I came here to talk business.'

Jacobs set down the bottle and turned around to face Powell. 'All right,' he said. 'Talk.'

'I want more money,' Powell stated.

Jacobs sat down behind his desk. 'You and Deborah are doing pretty well already. I think our contract with you was more than generous.'

'Yeah, well I'm sick and tired of living off Deborah's earnings,' Powell sneered. 'I want you to buy her management contract from me.'

Jacobs smiled, somewhat amused. 'What's this, Virgil? Trouble in paradise?'

'Never mind that,' Powell replied. 'I'm just not happy with this situation any more, and I want out. You'll get Deborah, and I'll get out of your hair, just the way you want it.'

'How much?' Jacobs asked.

'Five million,' Powell responded, speaking with the certainty of a man who knows he can't be refused.

Jacobs shook his head. 'You're out of your mind, Powell.'

'Am I?' Powell goaded him. 'I don't think so. Because in addition to Deborah Shain's contract, you also get a certain video tape I own.'

Jacobs looked at him steadily. Powell hadn't mentioned that video tape in ages; Jacobs had hoped he'd forgotten it by now. That video tape had changed their relationship completely. It hadn't been that long ago that Powell had been his employee; little more than an office boy, despite the fact he was in his thirties and had been working on the fringes of the music industry for years. Jacobs had never paid that much attention to Powell, not even when he started begging him to listen to a singer he'd discovered, a singer who, Powell claimed, was going to be the next big ticket.

Jacobs hadn't been interested in hearing Deborah Shain at all, until Powell got his hands on that video tape and started blackmailing him. Powell had forced him to produce Deborah's first album and push it with all the star-making machinery he had at his disposal. Fortunately, Powell's instincts about the singer's ability had been correct, and her album climbed rapidly to the top of the charts. Powell made a bundle off the album, and he stopped talking about the tape completely. Jacobs had hoped that as long as Deborah continued to make money for him, Powell would remain content and forget all about this blackmail business. He should have realized when he saw Powell's romance souring that it wouldn't be long before he came to him again, with new and more outrageous demands.

'That's still a ridiculous sum of money,' Jacobs said finally.

Powell laughed. 'Are you kidding? With all the money R-Jay Records is pulling in, you can afford that easily. You're making millions off Deborah alone.'

'Yeah, today, but who knows how much money we'll be making in a month or two?'

'I can tell you how much money you'll be making from the comfort of a jail cell,' Powell goaded him.

Jacobs visibly stiffened. 'Are you threatening me?'

Powell smiled. 'No threats, Neil. We're just talking a little business. I got the two things in the world you want most: Deborah and the tape. I'd say you're getting a pretty good bargain.' Powell pointed at the bracelet on Jacobs' wrist. 'You got trouble raising the money, why don't you sell that ugly bracelet of yours? That's got to be worth at least a hundred grand.'

Jacobs covered the bracelet with his hand. 'You're slime, Powell.'

Powell laughed aloud. 'Maybe, but I'm going to be rich slime.' He walked over to the window and looked out. From here, he could see Deborah sitting at one of the picnic tables talking to Jesse. He didn't like the way Deborah was leaning toward him, as if disclosing something of a confidential nature. He didn't like it at all.

'All right,' Jacobs said. 'I'll have the money for you

19

tomorrow morning. You bring in the tape, and the contract, and we'll settle this thing. And then you can get out of my life for good.'

Powell turned and showed Jacobs a nasty smile. 'Oh come on, Neil, admit it. You'll miss me when I'm gone.'

He laughed and walked out of the motor home, closing the door behind him. He stood on the steps a moment, watching the way Deborah was talking to Jesse. He didn't really want her any more; she was becoming too independent, too much her own person. He didn't like that in a woman. But at the same time, he wasn't prepared to give her up, not just yet. Until Jacobs came through with the money, Deborah was still his meal ticket. If Jacobs decided to be cute about this business and try to get out of paying him, Powell wanted to be able to take Deborah to another record company. She could still be worth a great deal of money to him.

So until he got the five million and could afford to leave Deborah for good, he wanted to keep her tied to him, frightened and intimidated. He didn't want her to have any friends or anyone she could go to for outside help or advice. And that's what it looked like she was doing now.

He strode angrily over to the picnic table and grabbed Deborah by the arm, almost pulling her out of her seat. 'Come on, baby,' he said. 'We're leaving.'

'But Virgil,' Deborah protested, 'what about the shoot? We need to do more takes this afternoon.'

'Well, your manager's wrapping it up for the day, okay?' Powell said intimidatingly.

'Hey,' Jesse interrupted, 'maybe she wants to finish her lunch.'

Powell snarled at him. 'What are you, President of her fan club? Mind your own business or I'll have security throw you off the lot.'

'It's okay, Jesse,' Deborah said as she rose to her feet. 'I really do have to go. I'm sorry we couldn't finish our talk.'

Jesse fished a card out of his jacket pocket and held it out to her. 'So am I,' he said. 'If you want to continue it, call me any time.'

Deborah reached for the card, but Powell was quicker.

He slapped the card out of Jesse's hand and it floated to the ground.

'I told you to get lost!' he shouted. He lunged across the table, but Jesse parried out of the way. Powell stumbled over the bench and fell, the front of his pants landing in Deborah's unfinished salad.

Powell scrambled to his feet and raised his clenched fists. Deborah quickly stepped in front of him.

'It's okay, Virgil,' she said. 'I don't even know the guy.'

Powell glared at Jesse, not moving. He pointed a threatening finger at him. 'I don't ever want to see you around her again! You got that, punk?'

Deborah's eyes pleaded with Jesse, begging him not to do anything. Jesse didn't speak; he just stood there on the other side of the table, returning Powell's harsh look.

'Come on, Virgil, let's get out of here,' she said, tugging on his arm. Powell was still glaring at Jesse, so he didn't notice as she surreptitiously bent down and scooped up the fallen card from the ground. Jesse noticed, however, and when she glanced up at him, a look of understanding passed between them. She was in trouble; she wanted to call him. Deborah stood up and continued tugging at Powell's arm, dragging him away from the table.

Powell finally allowed himself to be pulled away. Jesse watched quietly as the two of them turned away and walked toward Deborah's red Porsche, parked just beside the stage. Just before they reached the car, she turned back and gave him one last look. She seemed very frightened, and very lost.

Had Jesse been looking the other way, he might have noticed the two men stepping into Jacobs' trailer. And had he seen them, that might have changed the lives of a number of people. Not that there was anything particularly memorable about these two characters; they didn't look that much different from the other roadies circulating around the lot. The men were both big and broad-shouldered, with long dirty hair. They wore denim jackets and jeans, and neither one of them looked like bathing was a regular activity for him. The taller of the two, Randall Hooper, had a tattoo on each arm. His companion, Eddie, also had a tattoo, but it was in a place where only his ex-wife and occasional girlfriends had ever had reason to notice it.

The two men stepped into the trailer. Jacobs was at the bar, pouring himself another glass of Scotch. He turned around and looked at the two new arrivals.

'You wanted to see us?' Hooper asked.

'Yea,' Jacobs said, nodding. 'I'm having a little problem. I was hoping you boys could help me out.'

'What kind of problem?'

Jacobs smiled, trying to sound as casual as possible. 'Oh, something of a similar nature to that problem I had a few months back. You remember that, don't you?'

Hooper and Eddie exchanged glances and nodded. They remembered very well.

'You know, the last time we helped you,' Eddie pointed out, 'we almost got busted.'

Jacobs said, 'The last time you helped me, you also ended up with an extra ten grand in your jeans.'

'We talking about the same kind of money?' Eddie asked.

'I think maybe I can afford to double my stake this time,' Jacobs said. He sipped his Scotch while the two men considered his offer. He could see the greed in their eyes. The men were former motorcycle gang members, and they had had more than their share of run-ins with the law. Jacobs knew they weren't the sort to let legal niceties get in the way of scoring a lot of cash.

'What's the deal?' Hooper asked.

'Do you know Virgil Powell?' Jacobs asked, walking across the room.

'Yeah, I've seen him hanging around,' Hooper answered.

Jacobs looked out the window, just in time to see Deborah's Porsche disappear around the corner. Powell was a fool to think he could blackmail him for five million dollars. There were much cheaper ways of solving his problems.

'Mr Powell has something that belongs to me,' Jacobs said. 'I want it back.'

'And what do you want us to do with Powell?' Eddie asked.

'Oh,' Jacobs replied, sipping his Scotch, 'I don't want Mr Powell to annoy me ever again.'

THREE

'Who was that creep?' Powell asked.

He was driving Deborah's Porsche off the lot, while Deborah sulked moodily on the seat beside him.

'He was just this guy,' Deborah said, staring out of the window.

She clearly didn't want to talk about it, but Powell did not feel like letting up. 'He didn't look like "just some guy" to me,' he said. 'He looked like he knew you pretty well.'

'I just met him today,' Deborah insisted. 'Besides, he was a cop.'

Powell's eyes narrowed as he gazed at her suspiciously. 'A cop? What did a cop want with you?'

'Oh, nothing,' Deborah said, tired of all this questioning. 'He was just trying to talk me into doing this public service announcement for them.'

Powell looked disgusted. 'I already talked to those people about that. I talked to them a dozen times. I told them you weren't interested.'

'Well, that's what I told him, too. He just didn't want to take no for an answer.'

'I'm going to have to talk to a lawyer about that,' Powell said. 'What right do the police have coming around harassing innocent citizens?'

'He wasn't harassing me,' Deborah explained. 'He was just talking.'

'He was coming on to you, that's what he was doing. I could tell by the way he looked at you. Did he ask you out?'

'Of course not!' Deborah lied. 'But even if he did, why should you care? It's not as if we have anything great going for us any more. We're just roommates.'

Powell slammed on the brakes and turned to her savagely, pointing his index finger in her face. 'And we'll stay that way until I say it's over! Understand?'

Deborah nodded, totally intimidated. Powell started driving again and Deborah sank back into her seat. She didn't understand Virgil at all. He had long since given up the charade that he cared about her, but he still didn't want anyone else near her. She didn't know why she'd agreed to live with him in the first place. Their relationship had never really been that great.

Deborah had been singing at a club in the San Fernando Valley when she first met Powell. He came in one night and, after her set, he introduced himself as a personal manager on the lookout for new clients. He was very smooth and charming, bragging about all the important contacts he had in the music industry and convincing her she should let him represent her. It was only after she signed a contract with him that she learned he was not the big-time manager he'd pretended to be, but just a small-time hustler trying to make it in the record business. She was disappointed, even angry, but Virgil was so optimistic about her future that it wore off on her.

Then somehow Virgil pulled off a tremendous coup by convincing R-Jay Records to let her record an album for them. Their relationship was at its best while she worked on her album. But as soon as the album started selling, Powell began to resent her. The better it did, the more resentful he became. It was as if he were angry that she no longer owed her success to him alone. He started to denigrate her constantly, warning her that she was nothing without him and that she better not try to leave him.

His threats were effective only for a while, because she no longer felt she needed him. She was still afraid to leave him, however, not because she had any doubts about her own ability, but because she feared him and his near-homicidal rages. If she left him, she had no doubt he would come after her. And she didn't know what he'd do if he got his hands on her. So she waited, making the best of it, hoping that sooner or later he'd get tired of her and decide to leave on his own.

Deborah realized they were not taking the route home, and she asked Virgil where they were going.

'We're going to the bank,' he informed her.

Deborah looked down at the skintight costume she was still wearing. 'I'm hardly dressed for the bank,' she pointed out. 'Could you drop me off at home?'

'You can wait in the car,' Powell said, not even deigning to look at her. 'I'm going to the bank.'

She didn't feel like waiting out in the hot car, where every creep on the street could get a look at her. She followed Powell into the bank and waited impatiently while he went to get something out of his safety deposit box. She felt uncomfortable wearing such an outlandish costume in such a conservative atmosphere. Although she kept her eyes pointed down at the grey carpeting, she knew she was the recipient of more than one hostile stare from the men and women dressed in their Republican business suits, working at the desks in front of her.

A distinguished grey-haired man entered the bank through the door beside her, and as he walked past her, he smiled and said, 'Just get in from Mars?'

Deborah turned red. She didn't know why Virgil persisted in putting her through these kinds of humiliating situations. She didn't know why she put up with them, either. Fortunately, he came out a moment later. He had his leather shoulder bag strapped over his shoulder and whatever he'd taken from his deposit box was apparently already inside. She followed him out the door, still feeling every eye in the place trained on her.

'What did you get?' she asked innocently.

'None of your business!' he barked.

Deborah bit her lip, not daring to speak. It wasn't worth talking to him when he was in one of these moods. She climbed in the car beside him, and he drove off. He didn't say a thing, but she hoped he was heading for home

Powell was not unknown to the police. When Jesse got back to the station that afternoon, he followed a hunch and went downstairs to see if Powell had an arrest record. He did, and it was an enlightening one. Robbery, forgery, assault with a deadly weapon; he'd been arrested for them all. He'd served time on four separate occasions for assaulting women. He'd even been named as a witness several times in organized crime investigations. There was no question that Powell was a shady character.

Jesse didn't like the idea of someone like Powell being connected that intimately with Deborah Shain. He apparently had some kind of hold on her, and he was sure that violence or at least the threat of violence constituted part of it. And it was clear to him that Deborah wasn't happy with the situation and she wanted out. Jesse wasn't sure what he could do to help her, but he was determined to find a way.

He spread the file out on an empty desk and looked at Powell's mug-shots. From the side, Powell didn't look that different from the way he'd appeared that afternoon, but the look in his eyes in the head-on shot appeared dangerously psychotic. Jesse stared at the picture, so absorbed in it that he completely shut out all the noise and activity around him. He didn't even notice when Rachel Adams entered the office and stood over him, waiting for him to look up from the photos.

Rachel was an attractive woman (a few years older than Jesse) with shoulder length reddish-brown hair. Jesse didn't dislike her, really, but there were times when she could be a royal pain. She took her work too seriously and she never ceased nagging Jesse about some minor duty he'd neglected to perform. Jesse felt sorry for any guy who married her.

Rachel often wore outfits that showed off her figure to its best advantage, and today was no exception. She was wearing a bright green low-cut dress and high-heeled boots, which she was impatiently tapping against the tile floor, waiting for Jesse to acknowledge her presence. Finally, she could take it no more. 'So what happened?' she demanded, crossing her arms in front of her.

'What happened where?' Jesse mumbled. He picked up Powell's arrest record and studied it again.

'With Deborah Shain!' Rachel said, losing her temper. 'Remember? You were supposed to talk to her about doing one of the spots for us.'

'I remember,' Jesse said, showing her Powell's mug-shots. 'What do you think she's doing with a slimeball like Powell?'

Rachel looked at Jesse, totally bewildered. 'Who's Powell?' she asked.

'Her manager. Look at this,' he said, pulling out the arrest record. 'Four assault charges, all filed by women, and another dozen arrests that he never served time for. I mean, do you find that guy attractive?' He pointed at Powell's photo.

'Hardly. But I don't understand what this has to do with her doing the spot for us. What did she say?'

'She said she doesn't like cops,' Jesse said.

'Great,' Rachel moaned unhappily. 'I guess we'll have to write her off then.'

Jesse shook her head. 'I'm not so sure about that. I think this thing's a lot more complicated than it looks. I'm going to keep working on it.'

Before Rachel could reply, Police Commander Altobelli stormed into the room, waving a newspaper. Altobelli could never just walk into a room; he always barged in, shouting and perspiring and making accusations. He was a man with problems, as he never ceased reminding everyone around him. He had ulcers, he was starting to lose his hair, and the hair that remained was beginning to turn grey. He was a short man with shoulders like a football player's, and he always seemed to be gaining weight; his suits unfailingly looked about a half-size too small on him.

'Where is he?' Altobelli roared. 'Where's Mach?'

Rachel stepped aside so Altobelli could see him. 'Here I am, Commander,' Jesse said, raising his hand like a schoolboy confessing to writing a dirty word on the blackboard. 'What's the problem?'

27

'What are you going to do about Phil Simpkins?' Altobelli demanded.

Jesse looked confused. 'Who's that?'

'You're in charge of press releases and you don't even read the newspaper?' Altobelli threw the paper down on the desk and pointed to an article at the bottom of the page. 'Look at this,' he said.

Jesse read the headline: 'Police Not Protecting Public, Says Simpkins.'

'This guy's a plumber,' Altobelli explained, 'who's started his own police force, because he claims we're not doing our job. And the press is eating it up. He's making the whole force look bad.'

'Well, what am I supposed to do about it?' Jesse asked.

A vein started throbbing on Altobelli's forehead as he rocked back and forth, looking like he was about to strangle somebody. 'Your job is to make the department look good, remember? So talk to this guy and tell him to keep out of the papers.'

'I can't muzzle the press, sir.'

'You can try!' Altobelli shouted.

Jesse sighed. 'All right, I'll see what I can do. But I'm really busy right now.'

Rachel chimed in. 'Jesse's trying to get Deborah Shain to film one of the anti-drug spots for us. But he's not having very much luck.'

'He usually doesn't,' Altobelli said, giving Mach his usual vote of confidence. 'What's the problem this time?'

Jesse showed Altobelli the file on the desk. 'Commander, have you ever heard of a guy named Virgil Powell?'

Altobelli hadn't. Jesse quickly recapped his run-in with Powell that morning, and what he'd learned about him since. 'I think Deborah Shain's in some kind of trouble, and I think Powell's behind it,' Jesse explained. 'Maybe you should send someone over to have a talk with him.'

'Look, Mach, much as we may not like it, there still aren't any laws in this country against being a creep. I can't send anyone over to question Powell. As far as I knew, he hasn't done anything illegal.'

'But his arrest record—' Jesse started.

'—doesn't matter,' Antobelli finished, cutting him off. 'Look, if you can't get this singer to do a spot, you're just going to have to forget her. There's no point in wasting your time on something you can't do anything about. We have other, more important things to deal with here.' He waved the newspaper in the air. 'Like Simpkins!'

FOUR

A quarter-moon rose over the city. Downtown, the sky-scrapers exhaled their occupants, and the freeways filled with cars carrying harried office workers home to friends and family. Stars appeared in the sky, standing nocturnal guard over the people below. The sounds of day were gradually replaced by the sounds of night: crickets, dogs barking off in the distance, an occasional cry for help. In the warehouse district all was still. The massive storehouses, scenes of so much traffic and activity during the daylight hours, now stood quiet and abandoned. The streets stood empty after sunset, and a mangy cat walked down the centre of a throughway, dragging one useless leg behind it.

In only one building in the area was there any activity, and from its darkened exterior even that one seemed deserted. The building was solid brick and on one wall stood a yellowing billboard, advertising a brand of soft drink that had never been in existence. There was a row of windows beneath the roof, but on the inside, they were outfitted with blackout curtains to prevent the bright lights from attracting the attention of any overly-curious passer-by. There was no indication anywhere on the outside of who owned the building, or what it was used for, but it had stood here for so many years and been used by so many different people that the men who worked nearby had long ago lost any interest in its present occupants.

Norman Tuttle was hard at work inside the warehouse. Despite its plain exterior, the building was actually the Street Hawk Command Centre, and it was filled with extremely expensive and sophisticated computers and electronics equipment. Norman was busily making some last minute adjustments on the motorcycle's particle beam weapon, just one of a number of highly developed weapons he had built into the bike. Norman was a tall, skinny man with a receding hairline and a pair of deep-set eyes under dark and heavy eyebrows. He had his glasses on, as he usually did when he was doing close-up work.

Norman had made a few minor changes in the lower settings of the particle beam, and when Jesse arrived, he intended to send him out to perform some heat tests with it. Finally finished with the adjustments, Norman replaced the fairing, the metal plate beneath the windshield which covered not only the particle beam but also the twin fifty-calibre machine guns on each side of the front wheel and the rarely-used and occasionally unreliable rocket launcher. He stepped back and admired his work. Norman didn't know if his admiration of his machine merely reflected a father's typical pride in the beauty of his child, but as far as he was concerned, Street Hawk was the loveliest thing he had ever seen. The motorcycle was jet black, and totally streamlined, so that there was not an unnecessary ounce of weight to affect its performance. The suspension system automatically accommodated changes in road conditions and the airfoils had been adjusted to account for friction and air flow, allowing the bike to stop almost literally on a dime. Norman had built every feature he could imagine into Street Hawk to make it the best motorcycle ever manufactured.

He crossed the room to the Master Control Module, a huge computer console that covered almost an entire wall. He pressed a button on the console and a steel door came out of the wall, closing Street Hawk inside its pod, where the temperature was maintained at an unwavering seventy degrees regardless of the weather outside. Flashing lights winked at Norman as he regarded the computer console with pride. The computer was connected by phone lines to every computer and alarm system in a twenty-mile radius, allowing him to monitor the entire city from his chair. It also kept an ever-watchful eye on the motorcycle; nothing could happen to it without Norman knowing instantly. There were three video monitors in front of Norman's chair, the centre one of which was tied by closed-circuit video into the monocle targeting system inside Jesse's helmet, which meant that Norman could not only see everything Jesse saw, but record it as well. There were times when Norman, sitting in front of his machinery, felt he was riding Street Hawk just as much as Jesse was, and he certainly felt that he was as much in control.

He heard the door open behind him and he turned around. Jesse had just arrived and he gave Norman a friendly wave.

'It's about time you got here,' Norman said. Norman often felt that Jesse wasn't taking his responsibilities very seriously.

'I had dinner,' Jesse responded. 'Do you mind?'

Norman shrugged. He did mind, but he didn't feel like arguing with Jesse about it right now.

'What's up for tonight?' Jesse asked.

'Oh, I want to do those heat tests on the particle beam I was telling you about.' Jesse walked over to the console and Norman pointed out an area north of the city on the vector map above the video screen. 'That's the area I've selected for the tests,' he explained.

'Right.' Jesse went into the change room to suit up.

Normally, when Jesse changed into the black racing suit and helmet that marked his identity of Street Hawk, he tried to forget the ordinary problems that plagued his daily life. But tonight he had Deborah Shain on his mind. He couldn't stop thinking about her, worrying about her safety. He couldn't shake off the feeling that she was in danger. He was going to check up on her before he rode out to conduct Norman's tests, he decided. Norman wouldn't like it, but right now, he wasn't too concerned about what Norman liked.

When Jesse got out of the change room, Norman opened up the steel door that protected Street Hawk from the elements and Jesse mounted the motorcycle. He pulled down the full-length visor on the helmet, automatically hooking it up by closed circuit to Norman's console, and he said aloud. 'I'm ready.'

Norman heard him over his earphone and said into his mike, 'Let's go.'

Jesse started up the engine, and the wall in front of him split open down the centre, revealing the street. Jesse slid the bike into gear and turned the throttle. The motorcycle shot out of the building and hit the street, accelerating to a speed of fifty miles per hour in mere seconds. Behind him, the soft-drink billboard, the Command Centre's garage door, slammed closed, returning the building to its former, placid appearance.

Because a flashing, red light on the vector map indicated Street Hawk's position at all times, Jesse knew that if Norman kept track of his progress, he would immediately see he wasn't heading toward the test area. But he reasoned that if he was quiet, and didn't do anything out of the ordinary, Norman would just assume he was going the right way and wouldn't bother to check.

Jesse managed to speed through the city streets for a good ten minutes without Norman saying anything more than a warning about a car switching lanes in front of him. He would have probably made it all the way to Deborah's house if he hadn't gotten his directions confused and glanced up at a street sign to see where he was.

Spotting the sign on his video monitor, Norman said, 'Knollwood and Gothic? Mach, you're nowhere near the target area for tonight's test.'

'Relax,' Jesse answered. 'I just want to run by Deborah Shain's house first.'

'Do me a favour and check up on your dates some other time.'

'Deborah Shain isn't a date, Norman.'

'Then who is she?' Norman demanded, cutting him off.

'Don't you ever read "Rolling Stone" or listen to the Top Forty?'

'Not if I can help it,' Norman responded stiffly.

'Well, as the rest of the country already knows, Deborah Shain is the hottest thing to hit the charts since Michael Jackson. You have heard of Michael Jackson, haven't you?'

'Vaguely,' Norman admitted. 'But I don't see what that has to do with you. What do you want, her autograph or something ?'

'No, I just want to make sure she's all right,' Jesse explained. 'She's been hanging around with some bad company lately.'

'Of course she's been hanging around with bad company,' Norman countered sarcastically. 'She's a rock singer. Look, do me a favour, okay? Don't be a groupie on Street Hawk. Indulge your rock and roll fantasies in your own time.'

'I'm just going to cruise by once,' Jesse said, making a turn at the corner. 'It's right on my way.'

Norman looked up at the vector map above him. The flashing light indicated that Jesse was fifteen miles from the target area and proceeding in exactly the wrong direction. 'It's not even close,' Norman said.

While Jesse was heading for Deborah's from one direction, she and Virgil were heading home from the opposite way. To Deborah's surprise, Virgil had mellowed out later on in the afternoon. He had even offered, for the first time in months, to take her out to dinner. They'd gone to a fancy French restaurant, where Virgil had too much wine to drink and babbled to her about all the things he would do when he was finally a millionaire. He also informed her, in rather cryptic terms, that they would soon be apart, but that he hoped she would remember him with fondness.

'You weren't the right girl for me and I'm not the right guy for you, but we both got something we wanted, so let's not worry about it, okay?' he said, pouring another glass of wine down his throat.

Deborah tried to question him more closely, but Virgil wasn't talking. He just assured her that soon she'd understand everything.

All in all, it would have been a pleasant evening, except that sometime around dessert, Virgil decided the waiter was making eyes at Deborah. He lost his temper threatening in a loud voice to take the waiter out to the parking lot. Deborah came to the waiter's defence, but Virgil turned on her, too, calling her a string of vile names until the management finally had to ask him to leave. Deborah took care of the bill and they headed home. Deborah drove; she felt that Virgil was too drunk to drive.

When she reached their block, she noticed an old Studebaker parked across the street from their house and wondered briefly who owned it. She couldn't remember seeing a car like that in the neighbourhood before. Unfortunately, it was too dark for her to see Eddie, sitting behind the wheel of the antique auto, watching their approach with great interest. Otherwise, she might have realized something was wrong.

She turned into the driveway and slammed on the brakes when she saw Randall Hooper move out from the shadows beside the house and step into the glow of the headlights. He stared at the car, issuing a challenge with his eyes.

Deborah looked at Virgil. He had pulled himself totally out of his stupor and was frantically searching through his shoulder bag for something. He finally removed a manila envelope from the bag. As soon as Deborah saw it, she knew instinctively the envelope was what he'd taken from the safety deposit box that afternoon.

'Hold on to this, will you?' he said. He opened the flap on Deborah's oversized purse and dropped the packet inside.

'What is it?' she asked.

'My insurance policy,' he answered, grinning. He gave her a wink as he climbed out of the car.

'Virgil, wait!' Deborah cried, but he didn't pay the least bit of attention to her. He strode confidently toward the carport, while Hooper stepped out onto the asphalt.

The two men immediately started arguing. Deborah shut off the engine and rolled down her window, in a vain attempt to hear what they were fighting about. She was frightened. She'd never seen Hooper before, but she had a feeling he was dangerous.

Deborah could barely hear them, but it was obvious that Virgil clearly wanted the intruder to leave, and Hooper was refusing to budge. Hooper tugged on Virgil's shoulder bag, trying to get it away from him. Grabbing Hooper by the lapels, Virgil pushed him away. Hooper slipped over a grease spot and fell to the asphalt. As he got up again, he pulled a snub-nose .38 out of his jacket. Deborah saw it before Virgil did, and she screamed a warning, too late.

Hooper fired twice and Virgil fell to the ground. Utterly terrified, Deborah frantically switched on the ignition and the car roared to life. As she slammed the gears into reverse, Hooper raised his gun and fired at her. The bullet struck the windshield. Deborah ducked and pressed the accelerator down to the floorboards. The car screeched back into the street.

Jesse chose this moment to arrive. As the Porsche squealed in front of him, he jammed on the air foils and braked to a stop, missing the car by mere inches. Jesse caught a glimpse of Deborah's frightened face as she raced past him, but before he could turn to follow her, he heard the sound of a gunshot and felt a bullet brush past his shoulder.

He looked toward the house and saw Hooper running out on the front lawn, firing his gun at him. Turning his throttle as far as it would go, Jesse roared straight at him. Hooper fired once more, but the sight of Street Hawk bearing down on him like a fire-breathing dragon forced him to dive out of the way into the bushes. Jesse executed a perfect turn, carving a groove across the grass. He looked around for Hooper again and spotted him, just as he climbed out of the bushes and headed for the driveway.

Across the street, Eddie started up the Studebaker's engine and turned the wheel. Stepping on the gas, he hurtled across the street and up on the sidewalk, forging a path across the lawn toward the motorcycle. Turning his attention to the heavier foe, Jesse pressed a button on the display panel and the twin machine guns popped out. He cut loose with a spray of bullets, blowing out the front tyres

36

of the car rushing at him. Eddie lost control and the Studebaker careered across the grass, knocking over a mailbox before it skidded back into the street, grinding to a halt on its front axle.

Hooper had completely disappeared by now, taking Powell's shoulder bag with him. Jesse looked around for him a moment, and then turned back to the Studebaker, just as Eddie stumbled out of the car, hands raised. Jesse swept down on him and Eddie flattened against the car, nearly paralyzed with fright. Before he had a chance to question him, however, Jesse heard the sound of police sirens wailing in the distance.

'Get out of there, Jesse,' Norman shouted in his ear. 'Police ETA is—'

'I know, I know,' Jesse said. He wheeled away from the frightened Eddie and pulled back into the street. He could hear the sirens getting closer as he sped off into the night.

'We're not running that test tonight, Norman,' he said.

'I had a feeling.' He could hear Norman sigh.

'I've got to get back to the station. I want to hear what Altobelli gets out of that guy.'

Jesse found Altobelli sitting on a desk, watching Eddie's interrogation through a one-way mirror. Two detectives were grilling him and Eddie sat in a chair between them, looking from one to the other as they shouted questions at him.

'What was the gun doing in your car, Eddie?' yelled one detective.

'Why did you drive across the lawn?' questioned the other.

'Who killed Powell?' the first detective continued. 'Was it you?'

Eddie tried to remain calm. 'I'm not answering any more questions until my lawyer gets here,' he said.

'What happened, Commander?' Jesse said. 'I heard there was some shooting over at Deborah Shain's house.'

'Oh, you did, huh?' Altobelli asked suspiciously, shutting off the audio filtering in from the interrogation room. 'What do you know about it, Mach?'

'Nothing. Just what I heard over the police radio. What's

going on?'

Altobelli unwrapped an antacid tablet and popped it into his mouth. 'Somebody shot your pal, Virgil Powell. Killed him. And the only witness we got is this punk who claims he was on his way home from a date when Street Hawk attacked him.'

Jesse looked at the stoic Eddie, who still appeared unwilling to talk. 'He's lying. He knows something.'

'What makes you say that?'

'Street Hawk doesn't attack innocent bystanders. If he left him for the police, that means he was involved somehow.'

'Yeah, well that's what we figured, too. We'll find something to hold him on until we can get a better witness. Like Deborah Shain.' He turned away from the mirror and looked at Jesse. 'Any idea where we might find her, Mach?'

Jesse shook his head. 'None.'

'You know, I've been thinking about what you were telling me this afternoon. You said Powell was pushing her around. And he's got a long record of beating up women. Maybe he picked the wrong girl this time, and she shot him.'

'Don't be ridiculous,' Jesse said. 'Deborah Shain didn't kill Powell.'

'Oh yeah? How do you know? Were you there?'

'No, but I met the woman this morning. She's not the type to kill anybody,' Jesse insisted.

Altobelli looked disgusted. 'I'm surprised at you, Mach. You've been a cop too long to believe that you can spot a killer just by talking to him. Some of the worst killings in this country were committed by people no one believed were capable of it.'

'Maybe,' Jesse conceded, 'but I'm convinced this crime wasn't committed by Deborah. And if you give me some time, I'll prove it to you.'

'Mach, don't get personally involved with this. If you know where she is, tell me. If you don't, lay off the case.'

'Sir, Deborah Shain trusts me. If anybody in this department has a chance of finding her, I'm the one.' He emphasized his point by jerking his thumb at his chest.

'Mach, it's not your job to locate suspects. Your job is to

improve the image of this department in the public's eye. Your job is to deal with people like Phil Simpkins. Have you talked to him yet?'

'Not yet, sir. I haven't had time.'

'You see? Now, you take care of Simpkins,' he said, switching the audio back on in the interrogation room, 'and you leave Deborah Shain to me.'

'I'll do that, sir,' Jesse said. He didn't mean a word of it.

FIVE

The Fairworth Building catered almost exclusively to the entertainment industry. It stood twenty-four stories tall, in the high rent district over on the west side. Almost every office in the building housed companies involved in some capacity in providing music or films or television programmes to the public. Independent production companies, literary agents, personal managers, and entertainment lawyers populated the building's many offices. It was said that multi-million dollar deals were sometimes struck in the elevators and rest rooms, and more than one young hopeful had tried to get discovered by finding a maintenance job here.

The man stepping out of the taxicab in front of the Fairworth Building late that night did not look like he belonged in the entertainment industry. He was handsome in a rugged sort of way, and immaculately dressed in suit and tie; he appeared to be the sort who was never seen in public in jeans. He had pale blue eyes and an icy demeanour that indicated he could handle himself in almost any situation. When he paid the taxi driver, the hack refused to look at him; something about his passenger frightened him. The taxi drove off and the man looked up at the two dozen stories towering above him. There was hardly a light on in the entire building, but the man he was here to see was expecting him.

Carrying an impressive-looking metallic briefcase in his left hand, the man pushed through the revolving doors into the lushly carpeted lobby. The security guard sitting at the front desk looked up at his arrival and said, 'Can I help you, sir?'

The man turned his hard, cold gaze at the guard and then, ignoring him, walked over to the elevators and pressed the call button. 'You have to sign in, sir,' the guard pestered. 'It's after hours.'

The man said nothing as he stepped into the elevator. Protesting loudly, the guard jumped out of his seat but the elevator doors whooshed closed before the guard reached them. The man pressed the button for the penthouse and the elevator rapidly rose the twenty-four stories to the top floor. The door opened again and the man stepped out.

The name plate on the door in front of him indicated this was the office of R-Jay Records. The door was locked, but the man was adept at getting past such trivial delays and six seconds later, he stepped into the office. The reception area was dark, but he could see a light burning in one of the interior offices. He let the door close quietly behind him and waited a moment while his eyes adjusted to the darkness.

The walls were decorated with gold albums and silver-framed reproductions of album covers. Shag carpeting covered the floor and the furnishings were quite contemporary and very expensive. The visitor could tell that Jacobs was the kind of man who liked living well and would do anything to protect his ability to do so. That was good. It would make his job that much easier.

As he approached the lit interior office, he could hear Jacobs and Hooper arguing inside. Jacobs said, 'What I don't understand is why Eddie didn't go after her! That's what he was there for, wasn't it?'

'You didn't say anything at all about the chick!' Hooper protested. 'All you told us about was Powell. Besides, Street Hawk . . .'

'This has nothing to do with Street Hawk!' Jacobs shouted. 'You were supposed to get the tape back for me, remember?'

'I thought it was in his bag! You said he'd have it!'

'Well, he didn't! But I bet she does.'

The man stepped into the room. 'And this is the tape you want me to recover?'

The two men turned to him, startled. Jacobs was the first to speak. 'How did you get in here? I thought the door was locked.'

'It was.'

'You're Bingham?'

'Of course,' the man said. He seated himself comfortably on the white couch and placed his metal briefcase on the glass coffee table in front of him. 'Let's get down to business, shall we? Who is she?'

Jacobs picked up a thick file from the top of his desk. 'Her name is Deborah Shain. She's a singer. This is everything we have on her.' He handed the file to Bingham.

Bingham spread the file's contents onto the coffee table. There were press clippings, photographs, reviews, and the like.

'You just want the tape back?' Bingham asked. 'Or you want me to take care of the girl, too?'

Jacobs hesitated. He didn't like having to pronounce sentence on Deborah. But if she had seen the tape, he really had no choice; he couldn't permit her to walk around free. 'Kill her,' he said.

Bingham nodded. He gathered up the contents of the file and snapped open his briefcase. Hooper's eyes widened. Bingham's briefcase held an astonishing array of weapons: knives, pistols, a disassembled rifle, and certain chemical compounds used in the making of explosives. Bingham noted his look. 'Tools of the trade,' he explained. He dropped the file on top of his weapons.

Jacobs approached him with a bulging envelope and set it down next to the briefcase. 'That should cover your expenses,' he said.

Bingham picked up the envelope and looked inside. It was full of crisp, clean, one-hundred dollar bills. He didn't think it was necessary to count them. Jacobs seemed too scared to try to short-change him.

'What about Street Hawk?' Hooper asked. 'He gave us a hard time this evening.'

'If he gets in my way, I'll take him out, too,' Bingham said. He looked at Jacobs. 'Of course, there'll be an additional fee.'

'I don't care,' Jacobs said. 'I don't care what you have to do or how much it costs. I just want that tape back. And Deborah Shain dead!'

Bingham placed the envelope filled with money inside the briefcase and showed Jacobs a cold, thin smile. 'Consider it done,' he said icily. He slammed the briefcase shut.

SIX

The morning sky was clearer along the beach than it was in the smog-encumbered city. Already, the beachcombers were circulating along the sand, holding metal detectors out in front of them like lances, listening for the buzz that indicated they had located a cache of spare change or some equally valuable treasure. In the business district a few blocks inland, the small shops that catered to the tourist trade were opening for the day, the shopkeepers out in front of their establishments sweeping up the litter left from the night before. Legions of bored and unemployed youths stood outside their apartment buildings or roamed the streets, on foot or on bicycle or on skateboard.

A cool breeze wafted off the ocean, stirring the multi-coloured penants that advertised a sale at the local record store. A few teenage boys sat on a car outside the store, smoking cigarettes and listening to Deborah Shain's latest single, 'Golden Eyes', booming from the outdoor speaker. An attractive looking woman in a short skirt, her face hidden beneath a floppy hat and a large pair of sunglasses, sauntered past, and the boys whistled at her, one of them shouting, 'Hey sexy, you busy tonight?' The woman walked on without responding.

The boys would no doubt have been astonished to learn

that the woman they had just whistled at was Deborah Shain. She had spent the night in a small motel just a stone's throw from the beach, and early that morning she had gone out to purchase a few items that would disguise her appearance. Judging from the response she'd just received, she felt reasonably safe for the present. But she remained very frightened, and she hadn't yet decided what to do. The tape Virgil had given her the night before was still in the large purse she carried over her shoulder, and although she had not yet had time to look at it, she felt certain it was the reason Virgil had been killed. And she suspected as long as she had it with her, she was in danger also.

It would make sense for her to go to the police, but Deborah had hated and feared the police all her life. One of her earliest memories was of a half-dozen uniformed policemen bursting into her family's apartment and tearing the place apart, her father screaming at them the entire time. They had even gone into her room, cut open her teddy bear, and torn the stuffing out. Her mother had tried to repair it afterwards, without success, and Deborah could still remember crying herself to sleep for weeks afterwards because her family couldn't afford another one.

As she grew older and began to spend more and more of her time out on the street, the police always seemed to be hassling her and her friends about one thing or another. Every time she ran away from home because her father tried to beat her or her mother, the police would always bring her back. Deborah had tried to convince the police she was safer living on the street than she could ever be at home, but they were never interested in hearing her side of the story. She was a kid; her father was an adult. That meant her father was right.

It was hard for Deborah to change a lifetime of fear and hatred. Although she was an adult and presumably wiser than before, she still looked on the police as her enemies. She was as afraid of them as she was of the man who killed Virgil.

She heard a voice behind her yell, 'Look out!' and she jumped out of the way as a kid on skates sailed past her. She felt her heart beating madly. She knew she couldn't go on like this, scared of even her own shadow. She had to get help. Deborah reached into her purse and pulled out Jesse's card. She looked at it, considering. Jesse had seemed nice, a lot nicer than any cop she'd ever talked to before. Maybe, just maybe, he was worth trusting.

There was a pay phone on the corner. She stepped in, closing the door behind her, and put a dime in the slot. She dialled the number on the card and listened to the phone ringing on the other end. On the third ring, a woman answered. 'Officer Mach's desk,' the woman said.

'Is he in, please?' Deborah said, trying to hide the fear in her voice.

'No, he isn't. This is Officer Adams. May I help you with something?'

Deborah hesitated an instant, and then hung up. She couldn't leave a message for him. As soon as the police found out where she was, they'd come looking for her. Even if she talked to Jesse, he'd have no choice but to tell his superiors where she was. No, it had been foolish to call. Even Jesse wasn't worth trusting.

She started to leave the phone booth and then, thinking better of it, she went back in and closed the door again. There was still one person left she could count on.

She pulled out a dime and dialled another number.

The reason why Jesse wasn't at his desk was because he was at the Street Hawk Command Centre, searching through a stack of old record industry magazines. He was looking for any information he could find about Deborah Shain, anything that could give him some clue as to where she might have gone. He'd already tried the studio and the record company; they hadn't heard from her either, and no one seemed to have any idea what had happened to her. But Jesse was determined to find out.

Jesse had already warned Norman he wouldn't conduct any more tests on Street Hawk until he was certain Deborah was safe, so Norman, displaying a total lack of enthusiasm, volunteered his help. He never stopped reminding Jesse that he considered the whole thing a waste of his precious time, however.

'This is so archaic,' he complained, throwing a magazine on the floor and grabbing another one off the top of the stack. 'It would be so much easier if these magazines programmed their stories into a computer. Then all I'd have to do is punch in Deborah Shain's name and everything you wanted to know about her would pop up on the screen.'

'Great, Norman,' Jesse responded. 'You can work on that after we find what we're looking for.'

Norman continued in the same vein. 'This is going to take us hours, instead of the seconds it would take if we did it my way. Really, I don't know how people ever got anything done before they had computers.'

'We managed,' Jesse replied. He shook his head. This was so like Norman. He trusted machines implicitly; he had no patience whatsoever for any of the more human pursuits. Jesse often suspected that Norman was secretly trying to find some way to replace him with a machine, perhaps training a robot to ride Street Hawk, so he could eliminate the human element entirely from his work.

Norman sighed and pointed at the magazine in his hand. 'Here's something on R-Jay Records,' he said. Jesse looked over his shoulder while Norman read aloud, ' "Memorial Services were held today for John Raymond, President of R-Jay Records, who was lost at sea while on a fishing trip in Baja, California. His partner, Neil Jacobs, was unavailable for comment." ' Next to the article were two black and white photos, one of Jacobs, the other of Raymond, a good-looking man with streaks of grey in his hair.

'Anything on Deborah?' Jesse asked.

'Not yet. I'm still looking.' Norman scanned the article completely. 'Nothing,' he announced. 'It's all on R-Jay Records.'

'Well, try another one, then,' Jesse said. He took a fresh magazine off the top of the pile and Norman grabbed the one underneath.

'Hey, look who's on the cover!' Norman shouted. He read aloud, ' "Deborah Shain Hits Gold – Story on Page Twenty-Two." '

Jesse grabbed the magazine out of Norman's hands.

'You're welcome,' Norman said sarcastically.

Jesse flipped through the magazine to page twenty-two and ran his eyes down the article. 'Let's see, here it is. Born in Buffalo. . . . First started singing in New York . . . Owes her success to Artie Shank—'

'Artie Shank?' Norman cried, flabbergasted.

'Yeah, Artie Shank. You know, the old jazz musician. He's got a studio over on the west side.' Jesse continued to read.

'Artie Shank lives here in town?'

'Yeah. Say, did you know Deborah Shain used to sing with Shank?'

'Are we talking about the Artie Shank who did "Blue Rain" and "Serving Time"? '

Jesse nodded. 'Same guy. According to this article, he and Deborah were inseparable until he retired. I never knew that. Say, you know, we might have something here. Maybe he's heard from her or knows where she is. I think I'll go over and see him.' Jesse got up and started for the door.

'Hold on a second,' Norman said, rising to his feet. 'I'll go with you. I've always wanted to meet Artie Shank.'

'You? I thought you didn't like music.'

'I don't like rock and roll. Good music, real music, like Artie Shank, I like. Though I really find it hard to believe that Deborah Shain used to sing with him. There's no similarity at all between their two kinds of music.'

'How can you say that, Norman? Rock has its roots in rhythm and blues.'

'I can say that because rhythm and blues is music and rock is noise.'

'If you'd take the time to listen to some stuff, you'd probably like it.'

'I listen, I listen,' Norman insisted. 'I hear noise!'

Jesse opened the door to the street. 'Tell you what,' he said, throwing his arm over Norman's shoulder; 'I've got a tape of Deborah Shain's album out in the car. We can listen to it on the way over there.'

Norman winced. 'Must we?'

SEVEN

Artie Shank's studio was in a former warehouse district over on the west end of town. It had once been an industrial area, but rising property values had made such use prohibitive. Now real estate developers and self-styled trendsetters had made the neighbourhood their own. Old brownstone factories and warehouses were common here, and many a struggling musician or painter had sacrificed his life savings to move into this neighbourhood, hoping a more fashionable address would create the illusion of success that would give his work legitimacy.

Artie's studio was on the third floor of a four-storey brownstone. There was a ten year old Thunderbird parked across the street from the building with two men sitting inside it, watching the front door. Randall Hooper was behind the wheel, and C.L. Bingham, professional hit man, was sitting beside him.

Bingham made Hooper feel tense and nervous, and to hide his discomfort Hooper was reciting a very long involved story concerning a cruise ship, a long-legged waitress, a laundry room, two goats, and a crate full of bananas. 'So I follow her down there,' Hooper said, 'and there's these two goats in there, chewing on her uniform . . .'

'Mr Hooper,' Bingham said, cutting him off.

'Yeah?'

'Be quiet.'

'What?'

'Be quiet. I have a great respect for silence. You offend it.'

Hooper looked at his companion, about to respond, but Bingham turned his icy gaze on him and he changed his mind. He slumped down in the seat quietly.

Bingham didn't like the idea of having Hooper along with him. He didn't know why Jacobs had insisted, but he was the man paying the bill, and for that kind of money, the customer was always right. As long as Hooper kept out of his way, Bingham wouldn't fuss about him. Still, he usually preferred to work alone. The few failures he'd had in his fourteen-year career outside the law had been when he'd been forced by a nervous employer to bring some amateur along as a back-up. Although Bingham had never been caught, his back-ups invariably were, and he'd sometimes been forced to eliminate them himself rather than risk their talking.

Bingham felt he was the best in the world at what he did, and he regretted that in his profession skill was inversely proportional to fame. Bingham craved a little recognition for his work. He often wished he'd been born a hundred years earlier. Back in the Old West, professional gunslingers were not only well-known, but also well-respected. The law was a mere formality; the real rules were made by the smartest, the strongest, and the man with the fastest gun. And that was how Bingham saw himself: the man with the fastest gun.

A red Porsche turned the corner in front of them and Bingham sat up. He knew that Deborah Shain drove a red Porsche. He reached into his jacket and pulled out an H.K. automatic.

A car across the street from them was pulling out of a parking space and the Porsche slowed to a stop, waiting for it to leave. It stopped directly opposite the Thunderbird and Bingham could recognize the driver as Deborah even through her disguise. Her window was open and he had a clear shot at her. He raised his pistol.

'That's her!' Hooper yelled, pointing out of the window.

Deborah turned at the sound of his cry, and spotting the two men, she gunned the accelerator and skimmed around the car in front of her. Bingham jumped out of the Thunderbird and lifted his gun, just as Deborah disappeared around the corner. Frowning, Bingham returned the gun to its holster beneath his jacket.

'Come on, we'll go after her!' Hooper yelled.

'Not in this heap, we won't. She's scared. You're not.'

Hooper was confused. 'Well, what do we do then?'

'We wait,' Bingham replied quietly. 'She came to see Artie Shank once. She'll be back.'

'Are you sure? I mean, she saw us and everything.'

Bingham trained his icy blue gaze on Hooper once more. He'd had just about enough. 'Mr Hooper, your presence is no longer required.'

'Jacobs said he wanted me to—'

'When you work with me, Mr Hooper, I give the orders. Your presence is not required.'

Hooper frowned, but he was too frightened of Bingham to argue. He turned the key in the ignition but Bingham stopped him. 'Mr Hooper, I may have use for your automobile.' He held out his hand. 'The keys.'

Hooper reluctantly shut off the engine and handed Bingham the keys. 'So how am I supposed to get home?'

'Walk,' Bingham suggested.

Hooper got out of the car and slammed the door behind him. He started down the street, hunched over and scuffing his heels on the sidewalk, looking like a little boy sent home from the game because he was too young to play with the big kids. Bingham waited until he was out of sight, and then turned his attention to the third-storey window of the brownstone. The sound of a piano playing drifted across the sidewalk. Perhaps it would be a good idea for him to pay Artie Shank a visit himself.

Just as Bingham stepped into the street, he heard the sound of a Deborah Shain song in the distance. The music was getting louder and he stepped back up on the sidewalk just as Jesse's Mustang, the music blaring out of its speakers, turned the corner.

51

Jesse pulled into the just-vacated spot in front of the brownstone. Bingham moved a little way down the street, watching out of the corner of his eye as Jesse and Norman got out of the car. He had a feeling they were connected to Deborah somehow; their arrival here couldn't just be a coincidence.

Norman shut the car door behind him and looked up to the third floor. A sign hanging in the window read, 'Artie Shank Music School'.

'Look at that,' he said, pointing to the sign. 'Artie Shank's teaching. I can't believe it.'

Jesse said, 'Maybe he got tired of life in the fast lane.'

'But it's such a waste. I mean, a man with all that talent.'

'Hey, what better way than to pass the talent on. Come on,' Jesse said, starting for the building.

Jesse and Norman entered the brownstone and ascended the stairs. As the cool clean jazz sounds became clearer, a change seemed to come over Norman. He became excited, nervous, anxious; this was as big a moment for him as meeting Deborah Shain had been for Jesse. When they reached the third floor landing, Norman put his hand on Jesse's shoulder.

'You hear that? That's Artie Shank, playing "Blue Rain". I'd recognize his style anywhere.' He sighed. 'I remember the first time I heard him play. It was in a small club in Chicago, and I was with this girl—'

'A girl, Norman?'

Norman blushed and cleared his throat. 'Well, I was young. Anyway, the point of the story is, this is real music. Not like that junk you listen to.'

Jesse shrugged. 'It sounds just like rock to me.'

Norman shook his head as Jesse slid open the door and stepped inside. Norman followed him in and then stopped in the doorway, stunned.

Artie Shank was not playing the piano. The pianist was a young black boy, fourteen or perhaps fifteen years of age. Totally absorbed in the complicated piece, his eyes were intent on the sheet music in front of him. His playing was flawless and eloquent as he moved his fingers effortlessly over the keyboard.

Artie Shank sat next to the boy, his back to Jesse and Norman. He was nodding his head and beating his hand on the arm of the chair, keeping time.

The piano stood against a bank of windows, and the dust motes caught in the sunlight seemed to dance to the graceful rhythms of the music. The loft was huge, with brick walls and a hardwood floor. A curtain separated Artie's living quarters from the rest of the studio, and the few pieces of furniture in view were simple and tasteful. Adorning the walls was a gallery of old publicity photos.

The boy stopped playing, suddenly aware of Jesse and Norman's presence. Artie turned around. Jessie liked him immediately, even before he started to speak. He was in his mid-sixties, and the wrinkles in his face testified to the difficult years that lay behind him. But his eyes remained full of life and warmth, and he wore a gentle smile on his face.

'Good afternoon, gentlemen,' he said. 'I hope you have a good reason for interrupting this young man's lesson.'

Norman felt terrible and started to apologize, but Jesse cut him off. 'Deborah Shain,' he said.

Artie's smile grew wider. 'I have nothing but good things to say about that lady. I'm afraid you fellows wouldn't get any mileage out of printing that.'

'We're not reporters, Mr Shank. I'm from the police.'

Artie's smile faded. He turned to the boy sitting at the piano. 'We'll finish tomorrow, Anthony.'

The boy nodded. He shot a half-frightened look at Jesse and Norman, and then quickly gathered up his sheet music and started on his way out. At the door, he hesitated, turning back to Artie.

'What is it, Anthony?' Artie asked.

'How was I, Mr Shank?' the boy asked tremulously. 'Was it any good?'

'Good?' Norman said, before Artie had a chance to reply. 'We thought it was—' he looked at Artie, aware that he was about to blaspheme '—*him*.'

Artie winked at the boy. 'I never argue with a critic,' he said. 'It was just fine.'

The boy grinned. He slid open the door and thumped it shut behind him. Jesse waited until he heard the boy's footsteps tripping lightly down the stairs, and then he spoke.

'What can you tell us about Deborah Shain?' he asked.

'Deborah Shain's the best young singer I've heard in twenty years,' Artie said. 'May I offer you gentlemen some tea?'

Artie opened the curtain and Jesse and Norman followed him into the kitchen. While Artie put a kettle of water on to boil, he told them about Deborah.

'The first time I heard Deborah sing, I was doing a benefit at a girls' correctional centre in New York. We were playing "Homesick Blues", and I told the girls that if any of them knew the words, they should sing along. Well, a few of them knew the words, but Deborah's voice just rang out over all of them. The other girls stopped singing, and Deborah sang the whole song herself. I tell you, I never heard anyone like her. She was only seventeen, but she sang with the wisdom of the ages. I had her come up on stage and do a couple more numbers with us. She was really shy in those days, but real sweet, too. I think that was the happiest day of that girl's life.' Artie smiled with the memory.

'What was she doing there?' Norman asked.

'Time,' Artie answered. 'She'd run away from home a couple of times, she'd been caught shoplifting, a lot of worthless stuff. The kind of thing a kid does when she's out on the street and scared and hungry. They said they were locking her up for her own good.' Artie shook his head. 'It didn't seem like her own good to me. When she got out, she looked me up, and I made her a part of the band. She sang with us a long time. A lot of people used to wonder what a white chick was doing with Artie Shank. That was before they heard her sing. Then they knew.'

The tea kettle whistled. Artie turned off the flame and poured the boiling water into the three tea cups on the kitchen table.

Jesse said, 'Mr Shank, do you have any idea where we can find Deborah?'

'I don't know where she is right now, if that's what you're asking,' Artie said, handing Jesse a cup of tea.

'Mr Shank, Deborah witnessed a murder last night. It's very important that we find her.'

'I'm afraid you came to the wrong person. I'm not going to have any part of turning that girl over to the police. If Deborah doesn't want to be found, she must have a good reason for it.'

'We're trying to help her,' Jesse insisted.

'I never knew a cop who tried to help anybody.'

'So, that's where she got her attitude from. From you.'

'No. She had it before she met me. And she was right. The police never did her any favours,' Artie said, adding, 'Or me, either, for that matter.'

Jesse exploded with frustration. 'Don't you understand? Deborah's a witness to a murder! They're going to go after her next! Doesn't that bother you?'

'Of course it bothers me!' Artie shouted back. 'If anything happened to that girl . . .'

'Then help us. We're trying to protect her. I don't want to find Deborah with a bullet inside her.'

Artie looked at Jesse, considering for a long moment. Finally, he said, 'I heard from her this morning. She was supposed to be here—' he looked at the clock on the wall '—a half hour ago. She said if she didn't show up, I was supposed to meet her.'

'Where?' Jesse asked.

'My second home.'

EIGHT

The 'Limelight' was a small jazz club in the Valley. It had been there for years, nestled almost invisibly between two office buildings. It wasn't the sort of place one would ever think to enter if one were just driving past, but among true devotees of the local jazz scene, it was known as one of the few places in town to hear really first-rate contemporary music.

It was still early in the evening when Jesse, Norman, and Artie arrived. The room was dimly lit and a blue, smoky haze hovered over the bar. The few patrons in the club at this hour were quietly watching a young black woman at the piano. She sang in a searching, soulful voice as her hands eked out a slow blues tune. When she spotted Artie coming in the door, her eyes seemed to light up.

'She used to be one of my students,' Artie whispered to his companions. He moved forward and sat down at a table near the piano. Not wanting to intrude, Jesse took Norman by the arm and led him to the bar.

The woman came to the end of the song and the audience applauded respectfully. She smiled. 'Thank you very much,' she said. 'I'd like to play this next song for a very special friend of mine. Some of you might know it. It's called "Blue Rain".'

And she started playing. Perhaps her technique wasn't as

sophisticated as the boy Jesse and Norman had heard performing the same number that afternoon, but it was certainly more emotional, more heartfelt. She sang of hot summer nights and cool city streets and lost loves, half-remembered, and Artie's eyes welled with tears.

'That's why he teaches,' Jesse whispered to Norman. 'So his songs will live forever.'

Norman nodded.

The entire room was quiet as the pianist reached the final, brilliant arpeggio, and then the place erupted in applause. Artie's applause was the loudest, and the singer blew him a kiss.

Deborah entered the club. She stood in the doorway a moment, but as soon as she spotted Artie, she hurried over to his table. 'I was afraid you wouldn't come,' she said.

'Of course I came,' Artie said as he rose to his feet. 'I'll always be there for you, child. Don't you know that?' And then she was in his arms, no longer a big rock singer, just a frightened little girl, the same girl Artie had had to coax on stage the first day they met. She was trembling and Artie spoke to her in a soothing tone. 'It's all right, baby, it's all right. I know all about it now. And I brought some friends.'

Deborah looked at him, confused, and then turned around. Jesse and Norman were walking toward her. She backed away from Artie. 'What did you bring them for?' she asked.

'Because I trust them. They're here to help you.'

Jesse approached her. 'Deborah,' he said. She looked at him, for a moment wishing Jesse could just take her in his arms and make her feel soft and warm and protected. But he was a cop, after all, and in an instant, her plaintive look was replaced by a hard sarcastic sneer. 'I see you brought your partner,' she said. 'Where's the rest of the force?'

'He's not my partner. He's just a friend. He's not even a cop.'

'What do you want?' she asked.

'I want to know who killed Powell,' Jesse answered.

'I don't know. I don't know anything about it.'

'You were there, weren't you?'

Deborah stiffened. 'Yeah, I was there!' she said. 'What

57

are you going to do about it, arrest me? That's the bottom line with you cops, isn't it? You can't get the information out of her any other way, throw her in jail for a couple weeks! That'll loosen her tongue.' She held out her wrists. 'Well, go ahead! Snap the cuffs on me and take me away!'

'I'm not here to arrest you, Deborah,' Jesse said quietly. 'I'm here to make sure you're not the next victim.'

Deborah looked at him, still defiant. She turned to look at Artie and saw the gentle concern shining in his eyes. 'We're on your side, Deborah,' he whispered. She softened. Artie trusted Jesse, and she wanted to trust him too. Maybe, just this once, she could forget all her fears and prejudices.

'I don't know very much,' she said, turning back to Jesse. 'The man who killed Virgil, I never saw him before. But just before he got out of the car, Virgil handed me an envelope with a video tape inside. He called it his "insurance policy". I think that's what the man killed him for.'

'What's on it?'

'I don't know. I haven't had a chance to look at it yet.'

'Where's the tape right now?'

'I hid it in my car. I guess we could go get it . . .' Deborah started for the door and then stopped, frozen.

Bingham stood in the doorway, his imposing-looking automatic clearly visible in his hand. Deborah screamed.

Bingham raised his gun and fired, and Jesse shoved Deborah out of the way, just in time. The bullets whizzed past his ear.

The room exploded in panic as screaming customers scrambled toward the rear exit, knocking over tables and chairs in their mad dash to safety. The bartender ducked behind the bar and the two cocktail waitresses scurried into the midst of the rushing, frightened mob.

'Get her out of here!' Jesse yelled over the crowd as he pushed Deborah toward Norman. Norman stepped behind her, blocking her from the gunman's view as he pushed her into the rush of people shoving their way toward the fire door.

Eyes frantically searching for Deborah, Bingham turned his gun toward the crowd, ready to fire, it seemed, at random. Jesse grabbed a beer mug off a nearby table and hurled it at the hired killer. Bingham raised his elbow to ward off the flying glass and, forgetting Deborah for the moment, turned his attention on Jesse. He fired at him and Jesse dived to the floor, the bullet cracking into the wall behind him, splintering the woodwork. Jesse knocked over a table and ducked behind it as Bingham fired again. This time the shot drilled right through the table top, narrowly missing him. Jesse drew his own revolver as Bingham moved forward to get a clearer shot at him.

The room quickly emptied of everyone except the bartender hiding behind the bar, the two armed men and Artie, who had huddled behind a chair when the shooting first started. As Bingham moved in front of him, Artie slipped out of his hiding place, trying to sneak up on the killer from behind. Bingham marked his movement in the mirror behind the bar, and just as Artie reached out to grab him, Bingham stepped out of the way, grabbed Artie by the neck, and shoved him in front of him like a shield. He held his pistol against the black man's stomach.

'Drop it, cop,' Bingham said. Jesse moved out from behind the table, his revolver pointing at the gunman. The room was silent, save for the sound of their tense, heavy breathing. 'I said, drop it.'

'Not likely,' Jesse said. Sweat was starting to bead down his forehead.

'You can't shoot. And either way, I can.' He smiled confidently.

Jesse didn't move. He didn't have a clear shot, and Bingham could take them both out in a second. He couldn't take the risk. He slowly lowered his gun and let it drop to the floor.

Bingham moved toward the front door, dragging Artie along with him. Artie tried to pull away, but Bingham jammed the gun hard in his ribs. 'Don't try anything, old man,' he whispered. 'I want you alive, but you're not that important.'

Totally helpless, Jesse stood by and watched as Bingham kicked open the door behind him. The bartender stuck his head up above the bar, and the gunman quickly turned his weapon and fired at him, hitting the mirror behind him as the bartender dived back to the floor. Jesse started to reach for his gun, but Bingham was faster, and Jesse froze as the killer pointed his gun back toward him. Bingham pulled Artie out the door, and it swung shut after him.

Grabbing his gun, Jesse ran toward the door, but as he opened it, Bingham fired again, forcing the cop to duck back inside. He waited a moment and then, crouching down, he dived outside, landing on the sidewalk in front of the club and raising his gun to fire.

He was too late.

Bingham was jumping into a Thunderbird parked in front of the club. As Jesse ran over to his own car, the gunman peeled out and flew around the corner, too fast for pursuit. Letting his shoulders drop, Jesse returned his gun to his holster. He'd never catch up with him now.

Wearing a defeated expression, Jesse turned and went back through the nightclub to the rear exit. In the back alley, he found Norman and Deborah and the two cocktail waitresses. The rest of the customers had already fled to safety.

'It's all right,' he said. 'He's gone.'

While the waitresses headed back into the club, Jesse approached Deborah and Norman. 'Are you all right?' he asked Deborah. She nodded. 'Norman?' Norman nodded, too.

Deborah looked past him, toward the door. 'Where's Artie?' she asked.

Jesse looked at her, not speaking.

'He's hurt!' she cried, frightened. She started back toward the club but Jesse held her firmly.

'No, he's not hurt. He's . . . gone. Whoever that guy was, he took him.'

'Why? Artie has nothing to do with this.'

'He took him to get to you.'

Deborah drew her breath, letting this new development sink in.

Norman said, 'Jesse's right. They know Artie's your weak spot.'

'We have to do something!' Deborah said. 'Please . . .'

'What we have to do is find out who's behind all this.' Jesse drew his car keys out of his pocket. He threw them to Norman. 'Norman, you head home. I'll call you later.'

'What are you going to do?' Norman asked.

'We're going to take a look at that tape.' He turned to Deborah. 'Where's your car?'

'I parked around the corner,' she replied, pointing down the alley toward the street.

Jesse took her by the arm and they started to her car. Norman called after them, 'Don't forget to phone me. I might be able to help with my, uh, home video equipment.'

Jesse acknowledged this with a wave.

'Where are we going?' Deborah asked.

'Police headquarters.'

Deborah froze. 'No. Absolutely not.'

'Deborah, this is no time to be stubborn. This is the only way to save Artie.'

'You don't understand,' Deborah insisted.

'Yeah, I know, you had it rough. Well, lots of people have had it rough.'

'They'll lock me up!' Deborah cried.

'What?' He looked at her. She was trembling and looked like she was about to break down. He put his arm around her. 'Come on, Deborah,' he said, leading her to her car.

He took her keys, made her sit down in the passenger seat, and then climbed in behind the wheel. He waited patiently until Deborah got control of herself, and then asked, 'You want to tell me about it?'

'It's hard, Jesse,' she said. 'It's hard to talk about, and it's especially hard to talk about to you, because you're a cop. You see, all my life, cops have been nothing but trouble. Even from the time I was just a little girl.' And then she told him, she told him everything, things she had never told anyone besides Artie. About the police wrecking her home, about her father, the beatings, the hassling by the cops, the weeks she'd spent locked up. She told him about the time Artie had taken her out for coffee in a small town in New Jersey, and the police accused him of propositioning her.

'And then they took him out in the parking lot and

61

started beating him up,' she said. 'I tried to get them to stop, but they wouldn't listen to me. They just kept hitting him and hitting him.' She trembled. 'They left him there, lying in a puddle. He was in the hospital two weeks because of that.' Deborah looked at Jesse through tear-stained eyes. 'Now do you see? It's always so hard for people like you, who've never been in trouble, to understand. But the cops don't want to help people like me, or like Artie. They just want to use us, and if they can't use us, they hurt us. You take me to the police station and your friends will question me, and if they don't like the answers, they'll throw me in jail until I can give them answers they like better. And don't tell me it's not so, because I've seen it happen too many times before.'

'I'm sorry, Deborah,' he said softly, taking her hand between his own. 'I am truly sorry. But you have to believe me. I'm not your enemy. And the police aren't your enemies. There're good cops and there're bad cops, just like there're good people and bad people. I'm a cop. Do you think I'm so bad? Do you think I'm going to stand by and let them hurt you?'

'I don't know,' Deborah said. 'I just don't know what to think any more.'

'Can't you just trust me? Artie did.'

'Yeah, and where is he now?'

Jesse looked as if he'd just been slapped. He turned away and Deborah put her hand on his shoulder. 'I'm sorry,' she said. 'I didn't mean it that way. I know you tried to protect him.' She hesitated. 'I don't know who to trust or what to believe any more, Jesse. You better just do what you think best.'

Jesse reached over and gave her a hug. She smiled tremulously, and then settled back in her seat, looking worried and afraid. Jesse started up the car and headed for police headquarters.

NINE

The last time Artie Shank had had handcuffs on his wrists had been almost fifty years ago, when he was still a teenager. That time, the police had been his enemies. Tonight, he was hoping they'd be rescuing him. He was sitting in the front seat of the Thunderbird, which was parked beside a phone booth on a dark deserted street. Through the window, he could see Bingham talking on the phone. He didn't seem to be paying much attention to Artie and it occurred to him that it might be possible to make a break for it. Maybe he could get away before Bingham realized what had happened.

He reached up behind him and unlocked the door. Then, twisting in his seat, he grabbed the door handle and pulled on it. The door opened, but before Artie could push it further, Bingham turned around and looked at him. He cocked an eyebrow in his direction and patted his chest, just where his holstered gun was hidden beneath his jacket. The message was clear: one step out of the car and he'd kill him.

Bingham hung up the phone and walked back to the car. He opened Artie's door, locked it, and slammed it shut. Then he climbed in the other side and started up the vehicle. 'No more stupid stunts, old man,' he warned him. 'I don't want to hurt you.'

'Let me go and you won't have to,' Artie suggested.

Bingham smiled. 'Afraid I can't do that. Not just yet.'

They arrived at the Fairworth Building a few minutes later. As Bingham parked the car, he explained, 'There's a guard in the lobby here. We're going to walk in there, nice and peaceful. I'm going to sign in and you're going to look off to the side, so he can't get a good look at your face. You're not going to say anything or make any motions that will tip him off that something's wrong. Got it?'

Artie nodded.

Bingham unlocked the handcuffs, continuing, 'And just in case you get any bright ideas of trying to pull a fast one, let me warn you: if that guard gets the least bit suspicious, I'll kill him.'

Artie turned his head. 'What?'

Bingham smiled. 'That's right. I got you pegged, old man. If it's just your own life at stake, you might figure it's worth the risk. But there's no way in the world you're going to let some other guy get killed for you, is there?'

The old musician frowned and looked away. Bingham had indeed read him correctly. He couldn't take a chance, not when somebody else's life was threatened. And he didn't doubt for a second that Bingham meant exactly what he said.

Bingham grinned amiably as they entered the lobby. He sauntered over to the guard and greeted him in his most disarming manner. 'How you doing? Nice night, huh?'

The guard nodded. 'Seems to be, yeah.' He studied Bingham curiously, as if trying to place him. Bingham was counting on the hope that the guard's glimpse of him the night before had been so brief that he'd never realize he was looking at the same man. And from the guard's lack of reaction, it appeared his hopes were correct.

Artie looked off to the side, as Bingham had instructed him to do. Bingham signed in using pseudonyms for Artie and himself, and then taking Artie by the arm, he said loud enough for the guard to hear, 'Come on, George, let's go,' and led him to the elevators. They rode up to the penthouse and when they got out, Artie noted the R-Jay Records sign on the door. He knew that was Deborah's record label and he couldn't help but wonder what this whole thing was about.

Jacobs had left the door unlocked for them this time. They walked through the reception area into Jacob's private office, where the record company president was pouring himself a drink. He turned around and nodded a greeting to both of them. 'Drink, Bingham?' he asked.

Bingham shook his head. 'I don't drink.'

He looked at Artie. 'How about you?'

'I prefer to do without your hospitality,' Artie said snidely.

Jacobs shook his head. 'Friendly, isn't he?' he said. He walked over to Artie and looked him over, trying to get the measure of the man. 'So you're Artie Shank, huh?'

'If you brought me here to discuss business,' Artie said quietly, 'I think I should warn you that I'm very happy with the label I record for.'

Jacobs chuckled and sat down on his desk. 'Don't worry, Shank. It's not your music we're interested in. Your stuff doesn't sell, anyway.'

'What did you bring me here for?'

'Deborah has something I want. You're going to help me get it.'

Artie turned to the window and looked out over the glittering lights of the city. It was a clear night and he could see for twenty miles or more. It made him feel so insignificant. Life would go on without him. Music would still play, people would still fall in love, children would still be born. He'd lived a long, full life. If it had to end tonight, it wouldn't make that much difference. 'I'm not going to help you do nothing,' he said. 'I've lived long enough to know how to deal with folks like you, and there's nothing you can do or say that can make me play your game.'

'What game is that?' Bingham asked.

'You want me to call Deborah. And I ain't going to do it. That child's been through enough.'

Bingham smiled. 'You don't get it, do you, old man?'

'Get what?' Artie asked.

Jacobs explained. 'You don't have to do a thing. We didn't bring you here to call her.' Artie turned around to face his two adversaries. They were smiling confidently. 'We brought you here so she'd call us.'

While Artie was standing by the window in Jacobs' office, Leo Altobelli was sitting down to dinner. He had only arrived home a few minutes earlier, and his wife had heated up the leftover tuna casserole for him. He had just taken his first forkful when the phone rang. It was Jesse, calling from the police station.

'What are you doing calling me here?' Altobelli screamed into the phone. 'I just got home.'

'I've had a break in the Deborah Shain case,' Jesse explained.

'Shain? I thought I told you to leave that one alone. I said if you didn't know where she was—'

'I know where she is. She's right here, standing next to me.'

'Deborah Shain? You've brought her in?'

'Yeah,' Jesse replied.

'I'll be right down.' Altobelli slammed down the receiver. He started wolfing down the casserole on the plate in front of him.

'Don't eat so fast,' his wife admonished him. 'That's the reason you have heartburn all the time.'

'Jesse Mach is the reason I have heartburn all the time,' Altobelli grumbled.

Deborah and Jesse were waiting in Altobelli's office when he arrived. They had a book of mug-shots open on the desk in front of them, and they were slowly paging through it.

'Okay, what have you got?' Altobelli asked as he stormed into the office.

They told him the whole story: Powell's murder, the tape, Artie's kidnapping. 'We were just going through the book,' Jesse told him, 'hoping we could ID the guy that took Artie. But now that you're here, maybe it's time we had a look at this.' He held up the video cassette he had recovered from Deborah's car.

Altobelli nodded. Jesse had already brought the department VCR into the office. He slid the tape into the machine, turned on the television, and pressed the play button.

An image appeared on the screen: a rock and roll band with instruments in hand, getting ready to play.

'I know that group,' Deborah said. 'They're the Genetic Stumps. They used to record for R-Jay Records.'

A woman stepped in front of the camera, clapped the camera slate, and then moved out of the way. An off-screen voice yelled, 'Action!' and a moment later, the band started playing.

Three pairs of eyes watched while the band played an entire song. The music was dull, tedious, and quite forgettable, and the band was as exciting to watch as clothes drying. When the number came to an end, an off-screen voice yelled, 'Cut!' and members of the crew moved forward into the camera's range.

Deborah recognized a familiar figure. 'There's Virgil,' she said, pointing at the screen. Powell walked across the set. He leaned over to speak to the drummer, and then the screen went black.

'That's what you brought me down here to see?' Altobelli snarled. 'I'll admit it wasn't very good, but I don't think it was worth killing anybody over.'

Jesse looked sheepish and he was about to apologize when a new image appeared on the screen. 'Wait a second,' Jesse said, pointing it out to Altobelli. 'There's more.'

They turned their attention back to the television screen. The camera was in the same position, but the set was dark now, as if everyone had left for the day. Whoever had turned on the camera had probably done so by accident. Two figures moved into view and walked over to the band's equipment. They stopped right next to the drums. There was no sound and the men were barely discernible in the darkness, but from the way they carried themselves, it was apparent they were arguing about something. They stood by the drums for a moment and then they started pushing each other. One of the men fell over an amplifier and while he was struggling back to his feet, the other man pulled out a gun. A bright light flashed on the screen for an instant and then the first man fell back to the floor, unmoving. The remaining figure looked around and then hurried out of camera range. The screen went black.

Deborah sat in stunned silence for a moment, finally whispering, 'No wonder they killed Virgil.'

'Anyone you could identify, Deborah?' Jesse asked.

She shook her head. 'It was so dark. I really couldn't see anything.'

Jesse leaned forward and rewound the tape. He started playing it again, this time in slow-motion. 'Now watch closely,' he instructed her. 'See if there's anything at all here you recognize.'

They watched the shooting played out before them once more, and Deborah concentrated all her attention on the screen.

The bright light appeared again and Jesse said, 'What was that?'

'It was the gun firing,' Altobelli answered.

'I don't think so.' Jesse stopped the tape and played the scene back in reverse. When the light showed up again, he hit the pause button, freezing the image on the screen. 'See?' he said, pointing at the light. 'It's not the gun. It's further up on the wrist. It's a watch, or a bracelet.'

Deborah's eyes grew wider and she almost cried out involuntarily. She knew what the light was. It was a bracelet, a heavy gold bracelet, garnished with diamonds. She'd seen it a hundred times before, adorning Neil Jacobs' wrist.

'Any idea what that is?' Jesse asked her.

'Me? No, no idea,' Deborah lied.

Jesse let the tape play out.

Altobelli said, 'This tape is useless. You can't see anbody's face. You can't even tell what they're doing.'

'What do you mean?' Jesse explained. 'There's a murder right here on screen.'

'You don't know that. For all you know, they might have been two members of the band, rehearsing for their music video.'

Jesse replied sarcastically, 'Yeah, and maybe the guy that murdered Powell was just rehearsing, too. Commander, it's the only explanation that makes sense. Why else would someone try to kill Deborah, or kidnap Artie Shank?

'Whoever it is wants this tape.'

Jesse shut off the VCR. Altobelli sighed. 'I don't know. Maybe you're right. I just wish we could see those clowns' faces.' He pointed at the mug book, lying open on his desk. 'You have any luck with the book?'

'Not yet,' Jesse admitted, 'but we're still looking.'

'Why don't you go back to that? It'll probably be more profitable than looking at that tape a hundred times.'

'Excuse me,' Deborah said. The two men turned to her. 'Could you tell me where the ladies' room is?'

'Sure,' Jesse answered. 'It's down the hall, by the elevator.'

'Thanks,' Deborah said, standing up. 'I'll be right back.'

Deborah left the office and started down the corridor. She had already made her decision. If she identified Jacobs to the police, the next thing she knew, a couple of dozen policemen would be crashing into his office. They wouldn't care about protecting Artie; their only concern would be catching Jacobs and throwing him behind bars. And if Neil had been desperate enough to kidnap Artie in the first place, he was desperate enough to do far worse. She couldn't take that chance, not with Artie's life. She'd have to handle the matter herself.

There was a pay phone at the end of the corridor. Deborah looked back at the office she'd just left, to make sure no one was watching her. No one was. She fished out a dime, put it into the phone, and dialed the number to Neil's office.

Jacobs answered on the first ring. 'Hello?'

'Neil, this is Deborah,' she said.

'Deborah! What a coincidence! I was just talking to a friend of yours.' Artie, still standing by the window, winced at the sound of Jacobs' fake heartiness.

'Don't hurt him,' Deborah pleaded. 'Please.'

'Well, that's up to you, Deborah. You do as I say, and no one will get hurt.'

'I won't tell anyone about the tape! Honest!'

'Good. That's a step in the right direction. Now I'd like to arrange a little trade. Artie, for the tape.'

'How do I know he's all right?' Deborah asked.

Jacobs held the phone out in Artie's direction. 'Say

something, so she'll know you're okay,' he instructed him.

Artie yelled, 'Deborah, don't give them anything! I'll be okay!'

Bingham stepped in front of him. 'That's enough, old man.'

Jesse put the phone back to his ear. 'As you can tell, your friend is his usual cooperative self. Now, about this trade. I suggest we meet tomorrow afternoon, five o'clock, at—'

Deborah interrupted him. 'I'll pick the spot.'

'Whatever you want,' Jacobs conceded.

'How about . . . Silver Screen Studios? At the trailer?'

'We're shooting over there tomorrow. Won't it be a little crowded?'

'The more people around, the safer I'll feel. And Neil . . . no guns.'

'Of course not. No guns, no cops.'

Deborah looked down the corridor, toward Altobelli's office.

'Don't worry,' she said. 'I'll be alone. Like always.'

She hung up the phone.

Down the hall, Altobelli was hanging up the phone also. He turned to Jesse. 'They brought Simpkins in for questioning. Maybe now would be a good time to talk to him.'

'Who?' Jesse asked.

'Simpkins! The vigilante! Remember?'

'Right, right,' Jesse nodded.

'He and his crowd were giving some kids a hard time earlier this evening. We don't really have anything to hold him on right now, but maybe you could go throw the fear of God into him.'

'This really isn't a good time, Commander. I'm all caught up in this Deborah Shain thing—'

'All she's going to be doing is going through the mug book. I think I can handle that okay by myself.'

'You don't understand, Commander,' Jesse explained. 'Deborah usually doesn't trust cops. But she trusts me. And that means I can handle her better than you can.'

Just then, Rachel Adams stuck her head in the door. 'Excuse me, I didn't mean to interrupt anything, but I wanted to thank Jesse.'

'Thank me? What for?'

'Deborah Shain. She's doing the spot for us, right?'

Jesse shook his head. 'Wrong.'

'I'm sorry. When I saw her leaving the building, I just assumed—'

'You saw her where?' Jesse said, rising to his feet.

'Going out the front door. I just came back to get some papers—'

But Jesse didn't stop to listen. He tore out of Altobelli's office and ran down the corridor to the front door of the building. He stepped outside. Deborah's car was gone. 'Damn,' he muttered.

He stood out in the night air a minute or two, wishing he didn't have to go back in and face Altobelli. But there was no way out of it. He went back inside and slowly walked down the hall to Altobelli's office.

'So you can handle her a lot better than I can, huh, Mach?' Altobelli commented when Jesse came back in.

'Sorry.'

'I'll put out an APB on her. Don't worry, we'll get her back. In the meantime, I want you to go over to the Squad Room and have a talk with Simpkins. And when you're finished with that, you can come back here and look through the mug book yourself. You saw that guy too, right?'

Jesse nodded.

'Then get to it.'

'Yes, sir,' Jesse replied sullenly.

He ran into Simpkins just as he was getting ready to leave. Simpkins was a big, barrel-chested man in his late forties. He had light brown hair and rough whiskers, and he was wearing a blue windbreaker that had the words, 'Twelfth Street Protection Association', printed across the back of it, just above a picture of an American bald eagle. On his face was a look of extreme annoyance.

'Are you Phil Simpkins?' Jesse asked.

Simpkins regarded him dubiously. 'Yeah. Who are you?'

Jesse held out his hand. 'I'm Jesse Mach. Pleased to meet you.'

Simpkins looked down at Jesse's outstretched hand and made no move to meet it. Jesse put his hand down.

'What do you want?' Simpkins asked.

'I wanted to talk to you about—' Jesse read the words off the back of Simpkins' jacket '—the Twelfth Street Protection Association.'

'Yeah, well I just finished talking to those two guys over there,' Simpkins said, pointing to two uniformed policemen typing up a report on the other side of the room, 'about the Twelfth Street Protection Association. If you want any information, get it from them.'

'You don't understand,' Jesse said amiably. 'I'm not here to question you. I wanted to see if there was some way we could get your organization and the police to work together.'

'How's that?' Simpkins asked suspiciously.

'Well, you see, the way I look at it, we both want essentially the same thing: less crime and safer neighbourhoods. Now, the department has set up a Neighbourhood Watch Programme, so citizens can keep a watch on their own neighbourhoods and let the police know—'

'Oh, I don't want to hear this,' Simpkins said in a tone of disgust. 'You don't know anything, do you, Mach? You know why I was brought down here this evening?'

Jesse admitted he really didn't know anything about it.

'Let me tell you about it then, and you can see how useful your police really are. You see, there were a bunch of kids in our neighbourhood, high-school dropouts. They had started up their own little junior protection racket. You know, going around to stores, terrorizing the owners, maybe breaking or ripping off a few things, and then demanding money to leave them alone. If the guys didn't pay, the kids would hang out in front and scare away their customers or throw rocks through their windows at night, that sort of thing. Of course, I didn't know anything about it at first. I mean, I have a plumbing shop in the neighbourhood where I sell bathroom fixtures and stuff like that, but the kids were too smart to come around threatening me. They knew I wouldn't stand for it. Anyway, one of the guys, Marty Henry, he didn't want to pay, so he called the cops. The cops came down, they talked to the kids, but the kids denied everything. So the cops told Marty there was nothing they could do, and they left. And that night, the kids went to Marty's house, broke all the windows, slashed his tyres, and threw trash all over his porch. So Marty started paying them too. But he got sick of it after a while, and he came to us and told us the whole story. So,' Simpkins continued, smashing his fist into his palm, 'we had a talk with the kids ourselves. I don't think they'll be bothering anybody any more.'

'What did you do to them?' Jesse asked.

Simpkins laughed. 'Nothing. Of course, the kids claimed otherwise, but hell, they can't prove anything. Anyway, they're out of business now, and that's thanks to us, not the police. The police didn't do nothing. That's the way it always is. Either they can't do nothing, or by the time they show up, it's all over and the punks get away scot-free. Meanwhile, people are afraid to walk their own streets at night. They don't want their kids to play outside and they gotta keep their doors locked, even in the daytime. That's no way to live. So we're trying to do something about it. And you think we should join some "Neighbourhood Watch Programme"? ' he asked sarcastically. 'No thanks.'

'Mr Simpkins, taking the law into your own hands isn't any sort of answer.'

'Oh yeah? Well, it makes a lot more sense than waiting around for the cops to show up every time.'

'We're trying to help you,' Jesse insisted.

Simpkins chuckled. 'You want to help me? Then tell your friends,' he said, motioning toward the other policemen in the room, 'to keep out of my way.'

Simpkins turned around and walked out the door. Jesse didn't try to stop him. There was no point; there was nothing he could say to him. He didn't think vigilantism was a sensible solution, but in his own way, Simpkins was right. The police were failing in their duties. They couldn't protect ordinary citizens. Hell, they coudln't even protect Deborah Shain.

It was up to Street Hawk to do that.

TEN

There seemed to be a car lot on every corner in the South Bay. A drive down any of the main drags would take one past dozens of them, with cute names like 'Cowboy Bob's' or 'The Wheeler Dealers'. New and used, American and foreign, jeeps and vans, almost anything on four wheels could be purchased in this part of town, and at almost any hour of the day or night.

Deborah had decided to get a new car. A red Porsche was hardly invisible, particularly when every cop in the state would be out looking for her. And she was certain they would be, as soon as the police discovered she'd left. If she wanted to save Artie, it was essential she remain free until at least five o'clock the following afternoon, and that meant she'd have to get another car. As soon as she left the police station, she got on the freeway and headed for the South Bay.

She turned into the first car lot she saw, a small place with less than a hundred cars in sight and a big banner waving in the breeze, offering 'The Lowest Prices in Town'. The place was quiet; there seemed to be neither customers nor salesmen on the lot. But the big sign out in front was flashing invitingly, so she parked the car, got out, and waited for someone to show up.

A dark-haired man with a moustache and the least sincere

smile Deborah had ever seen in her life popped out of the office a moment later and hurried over to greet her. 'Good evening, ma'am,' he said with the kind of oily charm that made her skin crawl. 'What can I do for you this beautiful night?'

'I'd like to trade my car in,' Deborah explained.

The salesman looked at the Porsche, then looked at Deborah. 'This your car?' he asked, not quite believing that someone would want to get rid of a car like that unless it wasn't theirs.

'Yes,' she replied defensively. She reached inside and snapped open the glove compartment, pulling out the automobile registration. 'Here's the registration,' she explained, handing it to him. 'And if that's not good enough, I have ID to prove that's who I am.'

The salesman looked over the registration. 'Deborah Shain? The singer? Hey, I thought you looked familiar.'

'Thank you,' Deborah said as it suddenly dawned on her how she could make this deal quickly, with a minimum of questions. She blinked her eyelashes several times and ran her hand through her hair, giving the salesman the impression she was more than a little dizzy. 'You see, I was, like, at this party, right, and we were talking about cars and like my friends were saying that it was such a drag that everybody in the business was like, you know, driving the same cars all the time, like you know everybody I know has a Porsche or a Mercedes, and like it's getting really unhip, you know? So I said, hey, I'm like really sick of my car, right, and like maybe I should trade it in for a—' she looked down a row of cars, trying to pick out the kind that was most prevalent '—Chevy and like, all my friends said, "Oh no, Debbie, you're too chicken to do that," and I said, "Wanna bet?" so now they're like waiting for me and I want to trade this in and get back to the party so they can see I'm not chicken.'

While she spoke, she could see the expression of greed slowly wash over the salesman's face. He assumed she was totally stoned out of her mind and the smartest thing for him to do would be to make the trade as soon as possible, before she came to her senses and realized how much she was getting ripped off.

Twenty minutes later, Deborah was driving a three year old light brown Chevy Impala off the lot. She had been cheated badly, but the money wasn't a major concern of hers at the moment. She had received a thousand dollars cash in addition to the car, explaining to the salesman, that, 'none of my friends will believe I like really did it unless I at least have some cash to prove it to them.' She really got the money because she was almost stone cold broke but still had a couple more purchases to make before she went to her meeting with Neil.

Deborah was heading toward one of the roughest areas in town. She knew from her days of living out on the street, that if you had enough cash, you could buy just about anything, at any hour. You just had to know where to go. And Deborah's destination was a small and dirty motel in the red-light district, a place inhabited by pimps and prostitutes and drug pushers. Deborah put on her floppy hat and sunglasses again; she didn't want to be recognizable now.

She pulled into the motel parking lot and got out of the car. A slickly-dressed black man sashayed up to her and flashed her a smile, saying, 'New in town, baby?'

Deborah suggested he drop dead and then stepped into the motel office. She told the clerk she wanted a room and while she went through the charade of registering, she whispered to him, 'I wonder if you could help me. I need to buy a gun.'

The clerk was chewing gum. He didn't seem fazed by the question at all, but just kept moving his mouth at the same slow steady rate. 'This ain't a sporting goods store, lady,' he said.

'I know that, but I'm kind of in a hurry; I don't have time to wait for the stores to open.' She pulled a fifty-dollar bill out of her purse and set it down on the desk. 'There's another one of these for you if you can put me in touch with somebody who can help me.'

'I don't know anybody,' the clerk said, putting his hand over the bill, 'but I'll see what I can do.'

Within an hour, a man knocked on the door of her small dingy room. She opened the door and let him in. The man was small, with light brown skin and eyes that darted constantly back and forth as if on the alert for a threat from either side. He carried a large suitcase in his hand, which he set on the bed and then opened, showing her his display of weapons. He carried guns of all types: automatics, revolvers, and rifles. As she spread his stock out across the bed, he said, 'And if you want something you don't see, tell me. I can get any kind of gun you want, one day's notice.'

'No, I think these will do nicely,' she said as she tested the weight and feel of the various weapons. She finally settled on a small Sterling .22 calibre automatic. It seemed to be the lightest and the easiest one to carry around in her purse. The purchase set her back several hundred dollars, but she didn't care any more. The only thing she cared about was rescuing Artie. She didn't think she'd need a gun, but she wanted to be prepared, just in case.

The man left and Deborah locked the door behind him, slipping on the chain for double protection. She fell into bed, still dressed and utterly exhausted. She had one more purchase to make, a blank video cassette that she would use to trade for Artie's life. With luck, she might just get away with it.

She closed her eyes and drifted off into a deep, dreamless sleep.

ELEVEN

Jesse fell asleep sometime between three and four in the morning while looking over the mug book in Altobelli's office. Altobelli awakened him when he came in a few hours later and sent him off to his own office to finish looking through the books. The task took hours, confounded as it was by a constantly ringing phone, Rachel's inane requests for copies of month-old press releases, and Jesse's own mind, which kept wandering off to Deborah's desertion the night before and his genuine concern for her safety.

When he'd finally finished looking through the books, he'd come up with nothing. Zero. He could find no record or photograph of the man who'd taken Artie Shank. He went to Altobelli to report his findings.

'Are you sure?' Altobelli demanded. 'Did you look through all the books?'

'Every single one, Commander,' Jesse affirmed. 'And I studied every single photograph. He's not in here.'

Altobelli shrugged. 'Well, it was a long shot anyway.'

Jesse glowered at him, resenting the fact that he had made him waste hours on something even he admitted was a 'long shot'. 'How's the hunt for Deborah Shain coming?' he asked. 'Have you found her yet?'

Altobelli shook his head. 'No. She seems to have disappeared into thin air. But she'll turn up. They always do.'

'Yeah,' Jesse said. He spotted the video cassette lying on the edge of Altobelli's desk and picked it up. 'Do you mind if I borrow this?'

'That's evidence, Mach. Not very solid evidence, but still. . .'

'Come on, Commander. You know nobody here's going to look at it and I wanted to try watching it at home. I've got one of those wide-screen projection TVs. Maybe I can see something there we couldn't see here.'

Jesse's beeper went off, indicating that Norman wanted him to call in. Altobelli raised his eyebrows and Jess shrugged.

'My beeper,' he explained. 'I've got to call my service. I might have a hot date for Saturday night.' He waved the cassette in the air. 'What do you say, Commander?'

Altobelli replied gruffly, 'I thought I told you I didn't want you on this case.'

'Yes, sir.'

'But you're not going to get off it no matter what I tell you, are you?'

'No, sir,' Jesse admitted.

'Okay,' Altobelli relented. 'Just bring it back in the morning. First thing in the morning! Understand?'

'Right!' Jesse grinned. He flipped the cassette in the air and hurried back to his own office, where he put a call in to Norman.

'Hi, Norman. What's up?'

'That's what I wanted to know,' Norman said. 'You never called me. What happened with Deborah?'

Jesse told him the events of the preceding night. 'And I just got my hands on the tape, just this second,' he added. 'I thought I should bring it by to show you.'

'Great,' Norman said. 'Bring it over as soon as you can.'

As soon as he could turned out to be about an hour later. Norman was eagerly awaiting him when he finally showed up.

'What took you so long?' Norman asked.

Jesse shook his head. Rachel had been the cause of his delay, but he didn't feel like going into that right now.

'Never mind,' he said, handing him the tape. 'Here it is.'

'Good, good. I've been wanting to try this out for a long time.'

'Try what out?'

'You'll see.' Norman put the tape in his video cassette player. Jesse noticed it was connected to the computer console by a series of wires.

'Norman, sometimes I think the only thing you care about is trying out your new toys.'

'That is the only thing I care about,' Norman admitted.

He pressed the play button on the VCR and the image showed up on one of the computer console's video monitors. Norman ran the tape forward until he reached a point just before the two men started arguing, when both men's faces were on-screen and more or less facing the camera. He froze that image on the screen.

'Okay, now magnify by eighty percent,' Norman said to no one in particular as he twisted a dial on the console. He pressed a button and the image on the monitor grew larger. By adjusting a lever, Norman managed to centre the men's faces in the middle of the screen.

'It's still too dark,' Jesse said when the image ceased magnifying.

'Don't worry. I'll take care of that right now.'

Norman fed a series of numbers into the computer and pressed a button.

'You mean you can actually make this image lighter?' Jesse asked.

Norman nodded.

'When did you come up with this one?'

'I didn't. It was a couple of guys over in Defence. You know, for when they do recons, through camouflage or at night.' Norman smiled at him. 'We trade a lot,' he explained. He looked at the screen. 'Ah, here it goes.'

A grid matte appeared superimposed over the faces on the screen. The images began to go out of focus and the faces became a series of squares over various shades. The squares brightened in intensity and then faded out again, to be replaced by the men's faces again, this time sharp and crystal clear.

'Hey,' Jesse said, 'I've seen those faces before.'

'So have I,' Norman seconded, sounding a bit surprised.

Jesse looked at Norman, suddenly remembering where it was he'd seen those faces. He ran over to the stack of magazines they'd been looking through the day before.

'Thank goodness you never clean this place up, Norman,' Jesse said.

'I clean up. But that's your mess. You should have cleaned it up yourself.'

'Yeah, right,' Jesse said, flipping through one of the magazines. 'Here it is!' He walked back to the video screen, holding the article Norman had read to him yesterday, about the death of John Raymond. He held the two photographs next to the screen. 'There they are. Neil Jacobs. John Raymond.'

'So that's it,' Norman said. 'Raymond didn't disappear on a fishing trip. Jacobs killed him and then made it look like an accident.'

'Exactly.' Jesse nodded. Everything was clear to him now. 'And somehow, the video camera was turned on accidentally and caught the murder on tape. And Powell, who was working for Jacobs at the time, found it and was using it to blackmail him.'

'So Jacobs had him killed.'

'Right. And Deborah must have recognized Jacobs when she saw the tape last night. That's why Jacobs had Artie kidnapped. He knew as soon as she saw the tape, she'd get in touch with him. So Deborah's going to try to make a deal for Artie.'

'But we have the tape,' Norman pointed out.

'True. But Jacobs doesn't know that.'

'That means if we want to find Deborah—'

'—we've got to find Jacobs!'

Norman turned to the computer console and started typing in Jacobs' name. 'I'll have his address in five minutes.'

'And I'll suit up,' Jesse said. 'It's about time Street Hawk had a litle talk with Mr Jacobs.'

TWELVE

It was just past four o'clock. Jacobs paced nervously back and forth inside the R-Jay Records trailer. He stopped at the back door and checked for the fourth time to make sure it was still locked. Artie Shank was behind the door and Jacobs kept worrying that he might somehow escape before Deborah arrived.

He looked at the other two men in the room, wondering how they could be so calm. Bingham was sitting on the couch, reading a European fashion magazine, and Hooper was at the desk, playing solitaire. Deborah would be here in less than an hour, at which time Bingham would have to kill both her and Shank, yet the prospect didn't seem to bother him at all.

'Mr Hooper,' Bingham said without looking up from his magazine, 'I believe you're cheating.'

Hooper shot Bingham a resentful glance. 'Hey, it's solitaire! If I want to cheat, I'll cheat!'

Bingham smiled.

Jacobs turned away and walked to the window. From here, he could see the outdoor set where they were shooting the 'Monte Carlo' video. The set was supposed to resemble a European carnival scene, complete with fireworks. Booths had been constructed along a cobblestone street, and brightly-coloured flags hung all over the set. It was a beehive of activity, with the director shouting instructions to the jugglers and acrobats and fire-eaters who had been hired to give the scene the proper sort of ambience. Jacobs didn't like it. There were too many people around. There was no way they could get away with shooting Deborah Shain with such a huge crowd nearby.

'Don't worry about it,' Bingham had assured him. 'The more people there are, the better it is for us. Who's going to notice Deborah Shain with so much other activity going on?'

'Yeah, well what about the gun-shots?' Jacobs demanded. 'Somebody's bound to hear them.'

'They'll think it's part of the fireworks,' Bingham promised. 'Relax. Deborah Shain's a dead woman.'

But Jacobs couldn't relax, and he couldn't understand how Bingham and Hooper could relax, either. He walked over to the bar and poured himself a drink.

'You appear to be nervous, Mr Jacobs,' Bingham said.

'I'm fine, I'm fine.' He gulped down a swallow of Scotch.

'Perhaps it would be better if you were to go home.'

Jacobs turned to him. 'I can't do that. I've got to get the tape.'

'I don't think you have to stay just for that. We'll recover the tape for you.'

Hooper looked up from his cards. 'Yeah, boss. No sweat.'

'But I think I should deal with Deborah Shain myself. I mean, she knows me. She'll feel more comfortable dealing with me than she would with you.'

Bingham shook his head. 'Not if you keeping looking over your shoulder and trembling like a leaf, waiting for the gun to go off. As soon as she sees how nervous you are, she'll know something's up. I don't want her to get suspicious at the last moment and refuse to give up the tape.'

'You think I'm scared, don't you?' Jacobs said defensively. 'I can handle myself around guns. I killed Raymond, didn't I?'

'Yes, and you left behind a video tape of the killing in the process. If you'd left the job to a professional in the first place, none of this would have happened.'

Jacobs was stung by the criticism. 'You don't like me very much do you?'

'I never pass judgment on my employers. But just the same, let me remind you that you hired me because I know what I'm doing. Look at it this way. When your car has problems, you take it to a mechanic. When your toilet's leaking, you call in a plumber. And if you want to kill somebody, you hire a professional assassin. And just like you would with the mechanic and plumber, you tell him your problem and let him handle it the way he thinks best. You don't watch over his shoulder and tell him what to do the whole time. So I suggest you just trust me and let me handle this matter myself.'

'Maybe you're right,' Jacobs said, after a moment's hesitation. 'But look, I don't trust Deborah. She might be planning a double-cross. So when she gives you the tape, you take a look at it and make sure it's the right one.'

'Of course.' Bingham nodded.

'And get rid of the bodies someplace where they'll never be found. I don't want them turning up again in five or six months.'

Hooper said, 'Don't worry about that. We took care of Raymond's body all right, didn't we?'

'Yeah. Right.' Jacobs turned back to Bingham. 'And bring the tape by when you're finished.'

'I will. And then we'll settle payment.'

Jacobs nodded. He finished his drink in another swallow and set the empty glass down on the table. He looked at the two men. 'I'll see you later,' he said, and he walked out the door.

Driving home in his recently purchased Jaguar, Jacobs tried not to think about what would be happening back at the studio in less than an hour. He genuinely liked Deborah; she wasn't a slimeball like that creep Powell. But business was business and he really had no choice in the matter. Deborah had to die.

Her death was going to cost the company a lot of money. She was the biggest seller they had, and it would be difficult, at first, keeping the company afloat after the

84

'disappearance' of its hottest recording artist. Of course, Deborah had already recorded a few numbers for her second record. And with the rejected tracks from the first record, it was quite conceivable that Jacobs could put together enough material for a new Deborah Shain album. Those posthumous releases always seemed to sell well.

Jacobs' mind started clicking. There was a lot of money to be made from Deborah's death if he had the right aproach. He'd have to rush the album out, of course. The public was so fickle that within six months they wouldn't even remember who Deborah Shain was. He'd have to hire a good publicist, someone who could milk this disappearance angle for all it was worth. They could leak rumours to the press, questioning what really happened to Deborah Shain. Powell's shady past would serve him in good stead here. Powell's death could be made to look like a gangland slaying which Deborah had witnessed. That was just the sort of story that would keep Deborah's name in the headlines until the album was ready for release. Her fans would eat it up.

Jacobs chuckled to himself. With the right marketing approach, he could make a fortune. Poor Deborah! It was too bad she had to die, but there was no reason why he couldn't do his best to profit from her passing. And profit handsomely.

Jacobs turned into the long uphill driveway that led to his expensive and palatial home. On his way up the hill, he drove past the electric eye and the garage door swung open. He was almost at the end of the driveway when he saw the black-garbed figure wearing a helmet, sitting on an idling motorcycle inside his garage. He slammed on the brakes and the Jaguar screeched to a halt.

He opened the car door and stepped out onto the drive-way. 'Who are you?' he demanded. 'What do you want?'

'I want you,' Jesse answered, the microphone in his helmet modulating his voice to make it sound almost un-earthly. It was the sort of touch that always made potential opponents like Jacobs quiver.

'M-me? For what?'

'Murder.'

Jacobs' eyes widened in terror and he quickly jumped back into his car. He smacked the vehicle into gear and started backing out of the driveway as fast as he could go.

Jesse hit the particle beam and the laser shot out of the motorcycle, hitting the front of the car. The beam bent the grill out of shape and the bonnet flew open. Then Jesse hit a second button and fired a burst from his machine guns at the front tyres of the Jaguar. Speeding down the hill, Jacobs lost control as the tyres blew and he swerved off the driveway, crashing into a group of garbage cans on the front lawn. The rear end of the car fell off the kerb and came to a stop.

Jacobs jumped out of the car and started running down the street. Jesse throttled Street Hawk forward and hit the vertical lift button. The motorcycle sailed into the air, right over the Jaguar and landed in Jacobs' path. Jesse spun the bike around and Jacobs stopped dead in his tracks.

'Nice manoeuvre,' Norman said, watching the scene on his video monitor.

'Thanks,' Jesse whispered as he inched the cycle forward, toward Jacobs.

Jacobs stepped back. 'W-what do you want? What do you want from me?'

'Deborah Shain.'

'Deborah Shain? What makes you think I know where she is?'

'You know.'

Jesse kept moving Street Hawk forward, forcing Jacobs against the trunk of his car.

'I tell you I don't! I haven't talked to Deborah in two days! Believe me, the last time I saw her, she was shooting a video for us. But she didn't show up yesterday. I don't know what happened to her.'

'You're lying,' Jesse said. He pushed Jacobs all the way up against his Jaguar. He couldn't get past him now.

Norman suggested, 'Why don't you try a little good old-fashioned arm twisting?'

Jesse looked at the rear bumper of the Jaguar, locking the monocle targeting system on it. He pressed the particle beam and the laser shot out again, this time searing the rear bumper and splitting it in two.

Jacobs looked down and saw the chrome coming apart. Eyes bright with fear, he tried to move away from the car.

Jesse grabbed him by the collar and pushed him against the vehicle as the laser beam came closer.

'You're crazy!' Jacobs screamed.

Jesse did not reply. He continued to watch as the laser cut across the bumper. Jacobs' knees were right in its path.

'You wouldn't . . . please, you wouldn't . . .'

The laser was just a few inches away, and Jacobs howled, 'All right, all right, I'll talk!'

Jesse released the trigger, turning off the laser.

'Where is Deborah?' he demanded.

'She's on her way to Silver Screen Studios. She's supposed to meet with Bingham at my trailer over there. She's going to trade him the tape, for Shank.'

'And then what? They walk away?'

'No. Bingham's supposed to kill them both.'

Jesse gripped Jacobs' collar tighter and shoved him against the car. 'Jesse!' Norman admonished. Jesse loosened his grip, trying to hold on to his temper.

'What time is she supposed to be there?'

'F-five o'clock,' Jacobs stuttered.

'Jesse, it's five o'clock now!' Norman shouted.

Jesse let go of Jacobs and backed away from him. He whispered to Norman, 'When are the police due?'

'It'll be at least five minutes. I just called them.'

Jesse hesitated. He looked at Jacobs. 'Open up your boot.'

'What?'

'Your boot! Open it!'

Jacobs hurried to obey. In a second, the boot stood open.

'Now get in.'

Jacobs swallowed, but did as he was told. Jesse moved the bike around to the rear of the car.

'If you yell real loud,' he suggested, 'someone might hear you.' He slammed the boot closed. 'Norman, I need hyperthrust,' he said.

'I'm locking you in for Silver Screen Studios right now,' Norman answered.

He fed the coordinates into the computer. The machine automatically scanned the streets ahead, mapping out the fastest and most efficient route. The green light flashed above the hyperthrust switch, indicating that it was cleared.

'Counting,' Norman said as he hit the switch.

'Ready,' Jesse replied, looking down at the monitor in front of him. He watched the countdown on the digital readout, the numbers changing second by second. 'Five-four-three-two-one.'

Jesse felt the familiar sensation of the bike taking off under its own power. He could never quite get used to it; it was like riding a rollercoaster that had just been fired out of a cannon. His suit protected him from the friction of the air rushing past him as he zipped through the streets, accelerating at an incredible rate. He watched the digital display as his speed mounted higher and higher, approaching three hundred miles per hour. He would be at the Studios in mere minutes.

He just hoped he would be in time.

THIRTEEN

At five minutes to five, Deborah pulled over to the side of the road about a block away from the Silver Screen Studio. She popped open the glove compartment and pulled out the blank video cassette she'd purchased a few hours before. Ripping off the cellophane wrapper, she dropped the cassette into her purse, checking at the same time to make sure her gun was still there. It was. She started the car again and headed for the studio. She was ready for Jacobs.

The guard recognized her and waved her through the gate. She drove across the lot to the R-Jay Records trailer. She ended up having to park a little distance away from the Winnebago because a music video was being shot in the centre of the street. Deborah climbed out of the car and stopped to watch a minute.

It was the 'Monte Carlo' video, the same one Jacobs had been watching earlier. Music blared out of a loudspeaker system and fireworks shot off behind a set of buildings. The director was sitting next to the camera on a huge Titan crane above the set and shouting into a megaphone.

'No, no, that's not it,' he yelled. 'Cut, cut. We need more fireworks.'

Two days ago, the most important thing on Deborah's mind had been getting her video right. Now, she was walking around with a gun in her purse, a witness to a murder, wanted by the police, and trying to save the life of the man who had been closer to a father to her than anyone she'd ever known. So much could change in such a short amount of time. She wondered if her life would ever be easy again.

Deborah circled the set and approached the trailer. Hooper was in the back room, keeping one eye on Artie and the other one out the window. He spotted her as she neared the trailer.

'Here she comes!' he shouted to Bingham in the front room.

'If you hurt one hair on that child's head . . .' Artie began.

Hooper cut him off. 'We don't want to hurt her, old man. All we want is the tape. You just don't try anything funny and no one will get hurt.'

Bingham set down the magazine and walked to the front door. He swung it open just as Deborah reached the motorhome. Descending the two steps to the ground, he gave Deborah a broad smile. She didn't return it.

'Where's Neil?' she asked.

'He left. He's trusting me to take care of this little matter.'

Deborah hesitated. She hadn't been expecting this. 'Would you mind taking off your jacket?'

Bingham laughed, pulling off his sport coat. 'You see? No guns. Just like Neil promised.' He dropped the jacket to the ground. 'Now, where's the tape?'

'I've got it. But I want to see Artie first.'

Bingham called back into the trailer. 'Old man, come out here.'

Artie appeared in the doorway and stepped outside.

'You see?' Bingham said. 'He's okay. We're not monsters, after all. We just want the tape.' He held out his hand. 'Where is it?'

Deborah opened her purse and pulled out the blank cassette. She tossed it over to Bingham. 'It's all yours,' she said. 'Let's go, Artie.'

Artie took a step forward but Bingham put his arm out in

front of him, blocking his path. 'Uh-uh. First I look at the tape, then you can go.' He smiled at Deborah. 'Not that I don't trust you, Deborah, but it never hurts to be sure. Why don't you come in and fix yourself a drink while I have a look at it?'

Behind her, Deborah could hear the sound of music blaring over the loudspeakers again, and the fireworks going off. She swallowed nervously and reached into her purse, pulling out the .22.

'Raise them,' she said, pointing the gun at Bingham.

Bingham sighed as he raised his hands in the air. 'You're really not playing fair, Deborah.'

'Come on, Artie, we're getting out of here.'

Artie hurried over to join her. He glanced back at the trailer, just in time to see Hooper slide open the window and point the barrel of a gun in Deborah's direction.

'Deborah! The window!' he shouted.

Deborah wheeled around and fired her gun at the window. Hooper ducked to the floor as the window shattered, spraying glass all over him.

Bingham dived for cover under the motorhome.

'Run, Artie!' Deborah screamed. Hooper stuck his head back in the window and Deborah fired at him again. Artie grabbed her arm and pulled her away.

'Come on, child, we've got to get out of here.'

They turned and started running. 'That way!' Deborah shouted, pointing at her car on the other side of the carnival set.

Bingham crawled out from his shelter beneath the motorhome. He rushed back inside the trailer and opened his briefcase. 'You idiot!' he snarled. 'Who told you to pull out your gun?'

'But she was getting away!' Hooper protested.

'I had everything under control until you messed it up.' Bingham grabbed two deadly-looking automatics out of his case.

'Don't worry, we can still cut them off—'

'Just keep out of my way!' Bingham barked as he ran out the door.

Hooper paused a second. He knew what would happen if the girl got away. Jacobs would string him up and hang him out to dry. He ran out to try to stop them himself.

Deborah and Artie ran through the middle of the set, past a couple of gymnasts doing mid-air flips. Deborah side-stepped to avoid hitting the acrobats and instead ran into a juggler whose back was to her. He lost his rhythm and the set of dishes he was juggling crashed to the ground.

The director shouted at them over his megaphone, 'What the hell are you people doing down there? We're filming!'

Bingham, running up behind them, started firing at Deborah. The bullets struck the cobblestone street in front of her and she and Artie veered off to the right.

Members of the cast and crew screamed and started running in every direction as the bullets rained past them. Jugglers dropped their props, fire-eaters threw away their torches, actors tore apart the booths in total panic. Bingham stood on the far side of the set, trying to pick out Deborah and Artie amidst the rampaging crowd, but he couldn't see them.

'Don't worry,' the director shouted futilely over the megaphone. 'Those aren't real bullets.'

Deborah and Artie ducked into a side alley. They could see the Chevy, less than a hundred yards away, so near and yet so unreachable. 'Maybe we can make a break for it,' Deborah whispered between breaths.

They started across the road, but Bingham spotted them and resumed his gunfire as he moved across the set. Actors dived out of his way as he rushed past them. Deborah and Artie were forced to back off, and they turned around and ran in the opposite direction, down the alley.

When they reached the end of the alley, they were on Silver Screens' famed backlot, acres and acres of old movie sets as far as the eye could see.

'We can find someplace to hide back here,' Deborah said.

Artie paused to catch his breath. 'You go on ahead. When he comes after you, I'll try to slow him down.'

'I'm not going on without you,' Deborah said firmly.

'There's no point in both of us getting killed.'

'There's no point in either of us getting killed. Come on!' She tugged on his arm and Artie relented, following her into the maze of backdrops and makeshift buildings, looking for some kind of shelter.

Jesse retro-ed out of hyperthrust as he neared the Studios. The guard stepped out of his shed to flag him down and Jesse hit vertical lift, flying over the astonished man and roaring onto the lot. He sped through the studio streets at a velocity much higher than the prescribed fifteen miles per hour speed limit. Cars and shuttle buses braked to a halt and bewildered pedestrians jumped out of the way as he flew past.

On the streets in front of him, the director of the carnival video had descended from his perch on the crane and was walking through the set, trying to calm down the actors and extras.

'Everybody just take a deep breath and relax. They're gone now. Nobody else is going to interrupt us.'

Just then, Jesse tore across the set. The cast members screamed again and scattered out of his way. The director dived to the street as Jesse whizzed past.

He shook his fist at Jesse as he sped away. 'You're going to hear from my agent!' he shouted.

Jesse reached the trailer. The door stood open and Jesse shot up the stairs and through the door. He came to a stop inside the trailer and scanned the room.

'It looks empty to me,' Norman said, watching over the closed-circuit monitor.

'It is empty,' Jesse said. 'Which means they're someplace on the lot.' He turned the throttle and flew out of the trailer, kicking up dust and dirt as he hit the ground. He raced across the lot.

Meanwhile, Deborah and Artie had reached a set for an old swashbuckling film: a sixteenth-century castle that towered over their heads. The building was made of wood and papier-mâché, but it looked like stone. The flags on the battlements waved in the breeze and the gate stood open before them, beckoning. 'We can hide in here,' Deborah said, motioning inside.

They ran through the archway into an open courtyard. In the centre of the yard stood an elaborately constructed fountain, embellished with cherubs and angels. 'There,' Deborah said, tugging on Artie's arm and pulling him toward the fountain. They circled the fountain and settled to the ground on the other side, hidden from view. They were both out of breath and neither spoke for a minute as they tried to get it back. 'If we're real quiet,' Deborah whispered, 'he won't find us here.'

They waited for some sound of Bingham's approach, praying that it wouldn't come. Deborah found herself wishing the police would show up. She should have called them herself. She shouldn't have tried to handle this alone; she'd almost got them killed already and even now there was no guarantee they'd walk out of here alive.

She heard the drone of a motorcycle in the distance, but no police sirens, no sound of rescue. And then she heard footsteps walking through the archway. They entered the courtyard and came to a halt.

'I know you're in here!' Bingham shouted. His voice echoed off the castle walls. 'Why don't you just surrender?'

Deborah and Artie looked at each other, neither one of them making a sound.

'I don't want to hurt anybody!' Bingham continued. 'I just want the tape back!' His voice echoed in silence. Deborah and Artie could hear his footsteps as he walked across the courtyard, closer and closer to the fountain. 'Be sensible about this, Deborah!' he shouted. 'It doesn't do me any good to kill you if the tape's still missing! Our deal still holds! You leave Artie with me, you go get the tape and bring it back, and you both go free!' There was no response. 'Deborah, if you don't agree to these terms, that can only mean one thing. It means you can't get the tape and you don't have anything to offer me. And that means it's smarter to kill you both than to let you walk away. So what's it going to be, Deborah? Surrender? Or death?'

Bingham scanned the courtyard, holding his automatic

94

out in front of him, ready to fire at the first sign of movement. Suddenly, he heard footsteps behind him. He whirled around and fired into the shadows beneath the archway.

Hooper stepped into the courtyard, hands raised. 'It's me! It's me!' he screamed.

'You idiot!' Bingham shouted.

While he was thus distracted, Deborah and Artie made a break for it across the back of the courtyard. Hooper spotted them first. 'There they are!' he yelled.

Bingham whirled around again and fired at the fleeing couple. The bullets sang past them as they ran across the courtyard.

Elsewhere on the lot, Jesse slammed on the airfoils and braked to a halt. 'Norman, did you hear that?' he asked.

'Sounds like gunfire,' Norman said.

'Yeah. And real gunfire, not the movie kind.' Jesse spun the bike around and took off in the direction of the gunshots.

Deborah jumped through a window at the far end of the yard and pulled Artie through after her. The rear side of the castle was part of another set: the front of a blacksmith's shop on an old Western street. Deborah pointed at an old saloon with dusty windows and a pair of swinging doors. 'There!' she yelled. She and Artie ran toward it.

Bingham ran across the courtyard in the direction of the window on the far side, Hooper at his heels. Bingham turned around, shouting, 'Not after me! The other way! Cut off their escape route!'

'Good thinking,' Hooper said, nodding. He ran back toward the archway.

Bingham stuck his head through the window. Deborah and Artie were nowhere in sight, but he could see the doors in front of the saloon swinging back and forth. They had ducked inside. Bingham grinned. That was dumb, real dumb. They were already on the far end of the backlot and that meant the only way out of the saloon would be through the front door. And Bingham would be watching the front door.

Inside the saloon, Deborah and Artie were discovering

that they had indeed trapped themselves. The saloon was empty. There was no furniture, no bar, no place to hide. And no way out.

Bingham stepped onto the wooden porch in front of the blacksmith's shop and moved out into the dusty street. A couple of tumbleweeds rolled past him as he reloaded the clip on each of his guns. He slowly walked toward the saloon, a gun in each hand. He felt like the old-time gunslinger he sometimes imagined himself to be. There was no one to stop him, no sheriff, no rivals. He was the fastest gun in the West.

Hooper appeared on the far end of the street, on the other side of the saloon. Bingham motioned for him to stay right there. He planned to flush his prey outside and as Deborah begged for mercy, he would make her tell him where the tape was. And then he's shoot them both down like dogs.

He fired at the saloon window. It shattered and he could hear Deborah scream inside. He grinned with satisfaction and fired a couple more rounds through the broken window.

Jesse heard the gunfire. He screeched around a corner and banged to a halt.

Norman, watching on the closed-circuit monitor, could see a tractor-trailer hauling a massive brick wall across the road, blocking Jesse's path. 'No way around that one, Jesse. You'll have to find another route.'

'No, I don't,' Jesse replied, and Norman stared in horror as Jesse shot forward. He hit vertical lift and flew straight at the brick wall.

'Jesse, no!' Norman screamed.

Balsa wood and styrofoam flew in every direction as Jesse tore a hole through the centre of the brick backdrop.

Norman breathed a sigh of relief. 'It was just a set. Jesse, don't scare me like that.'

But Jesse wasn't paying any attention to Norman. He was racing onto the Western street, straight at Hooper. The gunman turned and fired at him. Anxious to find Deborah, Jesse wished to eliminate this minor threat as quickly as possible, so he punched a button on his console, launching a missile from the front of the bike. The rocket whizzed past

Hooper, striking a hay-loaded buckboard behind him. The buckboard exploded, and Hooper flew into the air, dropping his gun as he hit the ground.

Suddenly, Artie ran out of the saloon. 'Artie, don't!' Deborah screamed as she followed him through the swinging doors and stopped on the porch.

Artie scooped up Hooper's gun and pointed it at the groaning man. 'I got him,' he told Jesse. 'You take care of the other one.' He nodded behind him.

Jesse looked down the street. It was deserted. As soon as Bingham had seen Street Hawk, he'd ducked into the stable. This would call for a different approach, he'd decided. He was certain he could take Street Hawk, but he recognized that he was dealing with a more dangerous quarry this time.

Jesse slowly wheeled down the street, looking at the fake facades on either side of the set for some sign of Bingham. The assassin was watching him through the stable window, holding a gun in each hand. As soon as Street Hawk was past him, Bingham planned to shoot him down. He didn't like the idea of shooting a man in the back, but Street Hawk would be just as dead no matter where he was shot.

As he moved in front of the stable, Jesse slowly turned his head to examine it. Bingham ducked out of the window, waited a moment, and then looked out again. Jesse continued to cruise past. He hadn't seen him.

Bingham stepped toward the open door and looked out into the street. Jesse was just passing him now. In a second, his back would be to him.

Bingham rushed out onto the porch.

Street Hawk's automatic sensor noted the movement and flashed a warning on Norman's computer console. 'Jesse! Behind you!' Norman shouted.

Jesse shot forward, just as Bingham fired his guns at where he'd been an instant before. He turned the machine around and set off a round of machine gun fire, right at Bingham's feet. The bullets tore apart the wooden porch beneath him, and Bingham fell into the street. Starting to get up, he raised his guns to get another shot at his foe, but

Jesse fired first. The bullets whizzed past Bingham on either side, kicking up the dust all around him. Bingham didn't move. He could feel the rush of lead as it flew past his face, and the roar of gunfire seemed to surround him completely. Trembling, he sank back into the dust.

The gunfire stopped. Bingham looked up, staring at the black-garbed figure towering over him, silent, menacing, the sun glinting off his helmet. Guns hanging limply from his fingertips, the killer slowly rose to his feet. Jesse fired another round into the dirt, and Bingham danced backward, sobbing. He dropped the guns to the street and slowly raised his hands.

In the silence, Jesse could hear the sound of police sirens approaching. 'Let the police finish it,' Norman said.

Jesse looked down the street. Artie still held the gun on the unmoving Hooper, and Deborah stood behind him, gazing at Jesse with awe. They were safe now. 'Right,' he said. He gunned the bike around and sailed off into the sunset.

And in the centre of the Western street, Bingham stood, lonely and defeated. His guns lay in the dust beside him. He'd never realized what he was; he'd always been too good. No one had ever got the drop on him before, the way Street Hawk had. But now he had been tested, and he had failed the test. He'd looked into the depths of his soul and realized that he was, and always had been, a coward.

Bingham wept.

FOURTEEN

Jacobs told the police everything. By the time they had pried open the boot, he was a nervous wreck. He would have been willing to confess to plotting to overthrow the United States government if they'd asked him to. Instead, they merely asked him what had happened and he'd blabbed the whole story: killing Raymond, having Powell murdered, kidnapping Artie and hiring Bingham to kill both him and Deborah. He even told them how Bingham had been recommended to him and some of the allegations he'd heard about his previous activities. If the police could prove even half of the allegations were true, they'd have enough to keep Bingham behind bars for several lifetimes.

Norman picked up most of this information by listening in on the radio transmissions from the police officers who were bringing Jacobs back to headquarters. When Jesse got back to Command Centre, Norman relayed the information to him and congratulated him on a job well done.

'Yeah, it looks like Street Hawk had a pretty good day, doesn't it?' Jesse said as he took off his helmet. 'Of course, Altobelli's going to have a fit when he finds out Street Hawk's solved still another case for the Police Department, which means he'll be in a bad mood again in the morning, so I guess I lose either way. Oh well,' he continued, unzipping his racing suit, 'I'll see you later.'

Norman gave him a funny look. 'Where do you think you're going?' he asked.

'Home. Unlike you, Norman, I don't live here. I know you may find this hard to believe, but I actually do attempt to have something resembling a normal life. And right now, I'd like to go back to it.'

'I thought we could run those heat tests on the particle beam tonight.'

Jesse stood in the doorway of the change room, gaping at Norman. 'Tonight? Oh come on, Norman. I'm exhausted. Look, I've been all over the city today, I've been shot at, I saved two people's lives and put three dangerous criminals behind bars, and I did all this on only a few hours' sleep. Remember? I didn't even get home last night. I slept at the office. So I think the smart thing for me to do would be to take the night off and turn in early.'

Norman was singularly unimpressed by this argument. 'Jesse, granted, you may be a bit tired, but we're testing Street Hawk tonight, not you. Street Hawk's a machine, it doesn't get tired. One of the many advantages machines have over people.'

'Norman, you don't really want me riding Street Hawk if I'm not operating at peak efficiency, do you?'

'If we had to wait until you were at your peak all the time, we'd never get any work done, now would we?' Norman smiled. 'Besides, it seems to me we made a deal. You said that as soon as you made sure Deborah was okay, you'd do the tests. Well, just because it took you two days to make sure she was okay instead of the two minutes you thought it would take is no reason to continue to delay my tests any longer.'

'This is really unfair,' Jesse protested.

'It's perfectly fair,' Norman countered. 'We have a very good give-and-take relationship between the two of us.'

'Yeah. I give, you take.'

Norman sighed. 'You're not being very cooperative about this at all. When you get insistent about using Street Hawk for one of your personal problems, like you did the other night, I let you do it, don't I? I may grumble about it, but in the end, I always agree. So I certainly expect you to be available when I need you to do some of the real work around here.'

Jesse paced back and forth. He didn't want to sound childish about it, but he really didn't want to go out again that night. 'I know, Norman, and ordinarily, I'd just go out and get the tests over with. But tonight, I wanted to go home, shower, have a nice leisurely dinner, and maybe give Deborah Shain a call, see how she's getting along.'

'She's all right,' Norman assured him. 'I heard it over the police radio. Both she and Artie are okay.'

'Yeah, well I figured she was,' Jesse admitted, 'but I wanted to talk to her about something else.'

'What?' Norman asked, and then his smile broadened. 'Jesse, are you going to ask her out?'

'Well, yeah,' Jesse said, nodding.

Norman couldn't help but laugh. 'You told me yourself she's one of the most popular rock stars in the country. She can go out with anyone she pleases. What makes you think she'd want to go out with you?'

'Hey, I saved her life three times this week!'

Norman said sternly, 'Correction: you saved her life one time this week. Street Hawk saved her life the other two times. I don't want you blabbing any government secrets just to impress a girl.'

'I wasn't going to tell her anything,' he insisted. 'I was just pointing out that the idea of Deborah Shain going out with me is not entirely ridiculous.'

'Well, in any event, you're still going to have to call her in your own time. I want you to test the particle beam tonight. I don't like to have to pull rank on you, but if you insist—'

'Okay, okay,' Jesse interrupted. 'I can see you're not going to let go of this one, so why don't I just go ahead and get the tests over with so you can stop bugging me? But at least let me get some dinner beforehand.'

'I've already anticipated your request and had a pizza delivered while you were out. It's on the table over there,' he said, pointing to a table on the far side of the room.

'All right! At least you're using your head.'

He walked over to the table. Norman said, 'By the way, you owe me three dollars and twenty-nine cents for your share. That includes the tip.'

'Thanks a lot, Norman.' He opened up the white pizza box and his face fell. 'Oh no,' he groaned. 'Anchovies!'

FIFTEEN

Phil Simpkins' plumbing company was located on the corner of Twelfth and Lexington. It was a small, one-man operation and he had been in the same location for years. In the shop, he sold pipes, plumbing fixtures, toilet seats, and an occasional bathmat or shower curtain, but the major source of his income was service calls. Most of his calls still came from around the neighbourhood, but since so many of his former customers had moved to other areas of the city in the last few years, he occasionally found himself travelling ten or even twenty miles to fix a leaking faucet or a toilet that wouldn't flush. The customers he dealt with out in the suburbs often recommended him to their own neighbours, so his business continued to grow at a steady rate. He knew he'd never get rich from it, but he could at least support his family and most importantly, make sure his daughter Mary never lacked for anything.

Phil had never intended to be a plumber. As a boy, he'd learned the trade from his father and often went on service calls with him, but he'd decided very early in his career that it was not what he wanted to do with his life. He wanted something more, something exciting, something glamorous. So the day after he graduated from high school, he enlisted in the army. His parents were upset; his father had fought in World War II, and he didn't want his son to fight in another war. Now that the country was out of Korea, however, Phil thought another war was unlikely. 'But if there is one,' he told his father, 'I'm not the kind of guy to sit on the sidelines while other guys do the work. I want to be out there on the front, fighting for my country. And you'd want me there, too.'

Phil's prediction was wrong; there was another war. In the Fall of 1965, Phil was sent to Vietnam. He was a sergeant. By then, he had married Nancy, his high school sweetheart, and they'd had a baby girl. He didn't want to be separated from his family, but his country called him and Phil wasn't the sort to turn away from the call. He was a good soldier, quickly earning a reputation for guts and ingenuity. He didn't seem to be afraid of anything. Always on the front lines leading his men into battle, he found himself constantly volunteering for missions others were too cautious or frightened to accept. Time after time, he was offered promotions and time after time, he turned them down. He didn't want to be behind the lines, making decisions that would send other men to their deaths. If there were risks to be taken, he would take them himself. He accepted the medals and citations, but the promotions he always refused.

Risking his life like that on a daily basis finally caught up with him in July 1968. While leading an assault behind enemy lines, a shell dropped in front of him and exploded, wounding him and killing several others. He returned home with a Purple Heart and a body full of shrapnel. The government sent him disability cheques once a month, but Phil didn't like the idea of just sitting home all the time, waiting for a monthly stipend, particularly when he had a family to support. The only thing he knew, besides the military, was plumbing, so when his body healed, he opened up a shop and went into business for himself. He bought a house nearby, a small, white, one-storey home, with rose bushes in the front and a swing for Mary in the back. He liked the area; it reminded him of the kind of neighbourhood he'd grown up in, where everybody was friendly and it was safe to walk around at night. He was certain they'd be very happy there.

Phil eventually learned, however, that this wasn't the same America as the one he'd grown up in. Slowly, imperceptibly, over the years the news seemed to carry more and more stories about muggings, murders, rapes. The Simpkins family locked their doors at night and avoided strangers on the street, but they were certain it could never happen to them. Even when he heard about crimes occurring just a few blocks away, Phil still clung to the illusion that he and his family, at least, were safe. And then one night, they came home from a movie and found they'd been burgled. The television, the stereo, Nancy's few pieces of jewellery and silver were all gone. Even in their own home, they weren't safe from the two-legged animals who walked the streets.

That was the moment when Phil cried, 'Enough!' He had already fought one war for his country; if necessary, he would fight another. He got a few of his neighbours together, people who felt just as angry and distressed by the deterioration of the area as he did, and he formed the 'Twelfth Street Protection Association.' They roamed the streets at night, armed with baseball bats and whatever else they could find, looking for muggings and burglaries and other street crimes. When they found them, they stepped in and took care of the matter themselves. Crime in the area decreased and the Association expanded its membership. The word was out; this neighbourhood, at least, was no longer safe for the criminal element.

When Phil got back to the shop that evening after fixing Mrs McReady's clogged toilet, he found Carl Webber and his daughter, Sally, sitting in a parked car in front of the building. While he unlocked the door to his shop, Carl got out of his car and approached him. He was a small man with thinning hair and huge, owl eyes that looked at him through thick eyeglasses. 'Phil, can we talk to you a second?' he asked.

'Sure, but if it's not an emergency, I'd just as soon wait till tomorrow to fix it. You wouldn't believe the day I had. The things some people flush down their toilets . . .' He shook his head in disgust.

He noticed Sally climbing out of the car after her father. The small, thin, sixteen year old was wearing a ripped blouse and had a black eye. She looked very scared and upset, and Phil's jaw dropped open. 'Oh my God! What happened to you?'

'That's what we wanted to talk to you about,' Carl said.

'Why didn't you say so? Come in, come in.' The little bell above the door tinkled as Phil stepped in and switched on the light. Carl and Sally followed him inside, and Phil closed the door quietly behind them. The shop was small, with plumbing fixtures on display in every available space. Phil's desk was on the far side of the room, and on the wall behind it hung a selection of toilet seat covers. His workbench was pushed against the wall.

'Did you take her to see Doc Archer?' Phil asked.

'She doesn't need a doctor,' Carl explained, shaking his head. 'She's not hurt, just scared. Sally, honey, tell Mr Simpkins what happened to you.'

Sally turned her wide eyes to Phil, but seemed too frightened to speak. Phil tried to calm her down. 'Nobody's going to hurt you here, honey,' Phil said in his most soothing tone. 'Sit down and tell me all about it.'

Sally sat down in the chair in front of Phil's desk and Phil settled in the seat across from her. He opened the tiny refrigerator, just behind the desk. 'You want a soda, Sally?'

The girl looked at her father. 'Answer him, Sally,' Carl said.

'Yes, please,' she whispered.

'All I got's the diet stuff. I hope you don't mind.' He patted his stomach. 'Have to watch the old belly.' He handed her a can of soda. She opened it and took a sip.

'You want to tell me what happened to you, Sally?' Phil asked. 'Start from the beginning and take it real slow.'

Sally took a couple of breaths, as if working up the courage to speak. 'Well, you see, I was, I was walking home from school,' she said, speaking so softly that Phil had to lean across the desk to hear her. 'I was on Eighth Street and this car pulled up alongside me. There were these two guys inside, and they asked me if I wanted a ride. Well, I said no, but they said yes I did, I just didn't want to admit it, and then they drove the car in front of me, right up on the sidewalk. And one guy jumped out of the car before I had a chance to run and he said if I knew what was good for me, I'd get in the car. I didn't want to, so the guy grabbed me and pushed me into the front seat, and then he climbed in next to me so I was caught between the two of them.'

'Do you know these guys' names?' Phil asked.

Sally shook her head. 'No, they didn't say, but I've seen them around. They're part of that gang, the Savage Skulls. You know, they're the ones who wear the jackets with the white skull on the back.'

Phil nodded. 'Yeah. I've seen those punks around.'

'Anyway,' Sally continued, 'they took me to their head-quarters, one of those old stores over on Morton Street. You know the ones I mean?'

Again, Phil nodded.

'They made me go inside with them. There were about, I don't know, ten or twelve guys in there, and they were passing around a bottle of whiskey or something. And this one guy stood up and he asked the two guys why they'd brought me there and they said they just did it because they were bored and it was something to do. So this guy, Pug I think his name was, at least, that's what the other ones called him, he came over to me and he, he—' Sally stopped, unable to continue.

Phil looked at Carl with a question in his eyes. 'Tell Mr Simpkins what he did to you, honey,' her father said.

Sally started to cry. 'He put his hands on me. He just started touching me all over and he was laughing and he told the other guys I was too skinny, he liked his girls with more meat on them. I tried to get away from him, so he ripped my blouse and everyone laughed, and I screamed and he hit me. That's how I got the black eye.'

She was sobbing louder now. Phil handed her a Kleenex and she blew her nose. The girl's father looked ill.

'They all made a circle around me and they started telling me these things they wanted me to do. All kinds of horrible things.' She started shaking. 'I was crying and they were all laughing at me, and the more I cried, the more they laughed. So finally Pug said if all I was going to do was cry, I wasn't going to be any fun, so they sent me home.'

Carl said, 'Linda wanted me to call the police, but I figured, what the hell, they're not going to do anything. So I brought her here.'

Phil leaned over and said, 'You're okay, Sally? You don't need to see a doctor or anything?'

'They didn't do anything except hit me,' Sally answered. 'I'm okay.'

'Good. Now listen. I'm gonna call some friends of mine and we're gonna go over and see those guys who bothered you this afternoon. We're gonna teach them that they can't start picking up girls off the street and scaring them like that. They ain't gonna get away with that kind of thing, not in this neighbourhood. But I need you to help me, Sally. I want you to come with us and show us the building they took you to. You think you can do that?'

Sally nodded. She wiped the tears off her cheeks.

'Good.' He picked up the phone and began to dial a number. He'd call the other members of the Association in a moment, but first he had to talk to his wife.

'Nancy,' he said, when she answered the phone. 'I'm going to be a little late for dinner tonight.'

SIXTEEN

Some nights are quiet. Some nights are not. This was not shaping up to be a quiet night for either Phil Simpkins or George Scroope, although Scroope didn't know it yet. He was a security guard at a federal depository and he was a bit nervous this evening, because there was more than a ton of gold stored in the huge vault in the back of the building. He never felt comfortable when he stood watch over gold. He'd worked here for more than twenty years and although he'd guarded almost everything of value at one time or another during his career, it was only when there was gold in the vault that it ever occurred to him something untoward might happen. Not that anything ever had. In all the years, there had not been one single robbery, and only a few half-hearted attempts. George wanted his record to remain intact until the day he retired. Still, he would feel a lot better tomorrow, when the truck came that would take the gold to Denver.

The building was protected by an efficient alarm system. Every door, every window in the entire place was hooked into the system, which meant no one could go in or out until George turned off the alarm. The building was secure even without George's presence; he was here basically as a back-up, in case something went wrong with the system or there was a power failure. It was too dangerous to leave objects of such extreme value locked up at night with only electronics to protect them.

George sat at a desk just inside the door, reading an Agatha Christie mystery and looking up from time to time to check the street. Once every twenty minutes, he took a walk around the premises, checking all the doors and windows, looking in every room, just to make sure nothing was wrong. When he came back to his desk after his latest survey of the premises, he noticed a man smoking a cigarette standing by the lamp post in front of the building. The man had his back to him, but from the way he checked his watch every couple of minutes, George assumed he was just waiting for somebody to pick him up. George went back to his reading but while he was absorbed in the book, he heard a groan from outside and looked up, just in time to see the man grip his chest and fall to the street. George stood up and ran to the door. The man lay in the gutter, not moving. George scurried back to his desk to call an ambulance, but then he hesitated. It would take at least ten minutes for help to arrive. By then, the man could be dead. George was trained in CPR; it was quite possible he could save the man's life if he got to him in time. He wasn't supposed to open the front door, not to anybody, until seven-thirty in the morning when the day guard came on to relieve him. But a man's life was at stake. George really had no choice.

He opened the master control board for the alarm system. There were separate alarms for every door and George shut off the one for the front of the building. He unlocked the front door and ran outside, bending over the prone figure in the street.

'Are you all right?' he asked.

The man didn't move, but the door of the black van parked right in front of him did. It slid open and George looked up to find himself staring into the twin barrels of a twelve-gauge shotgun. The man holding the gun wore a nylon stocking over his head and there were two men disguised in the same manner standing in the van behind him.

George raised his hands and slowly stood up as the three men jumped out of the back of the van. One of them

110

stepped behind him and removed his gun from his holster, and then the man with the shotgun nodded to the door and George led his three assailants inside. As soon as they were out of sight, the man in the gutter stood up and wiped himself off. He was a handsome man, with dark hair and a ruthless temperament. His name was Henri Dumos.

Dumos slipped his own nylon mask over his head and went inside to join his men. Albert, the man with the shotgun, was Dumos' second-in-command, and when Dumos stepped in, Albert asked him where they were going.

'The back,' Dumos said, and he led his men and their helpless victim to the huge wall-sized vault in the back room. There was a gate of heavy iron bars in front of the vault, and Dumos instructed the guard to open it.

George unlocked the gate and swung it open. 'You know,' he pointed out, 'this isn't going to do you any good. I can't open the vault. It's on a timer. It can't be opened until tomorrow morning.'

'Yes it can,' Dumos said. He nodded to the man standing behind Scroope and the man struck him over the head with a blackjack. George crumpled to the floor.

'Tie him up and get him out of the way,' Dumos instructed, 'while we take care of the safe.'

The man dragged George over to the wall and began to bind him with some heavy cord he pulled out of his jacket. While he was thus engaged, Albert ran back out to the van and returned a moment later with a magnetic explosive device. Dumos smiled with satisfaction. Everything was going like clockwork. But then, all of Dumos' plans went like clockwork. That's why he was so successful; Dumos was a great believer in the schedules. He always did thorough research before he committed a robbery and prepared for any eventuality, anything that might interfere with his plans. Like tonight. He'd predicted Scroope would unlock the door within sixty seconds after he staged the heart attack, and he'd been right. He'd learned a lot about Scroope over the past few weeks. He knew he was the sort of man who would unlock the door if he thought a man's life was at stake. That was the key, to know how people would react.

And since he'd been successful so far, he had no reason to doubt the rest of the robbery would proceed as expected.

Dumos waited as Albert and the other two men locked the explosive around the vault handle, just as they'd done in the practice sessions he'd had them stage. Albert ran the electrical wires through the charge and, after double-checking to make sure the wires were firmly attached to the timer, he nodded to Dumos. Stepping forward, Dumos took one fast look over the device himself, and then set the timer for one minute. The four men quickly separated, ducking behind furniture and around corners, away from the vault door. Peeking out from his hiding space behind a desk, Dumos watched the timer as the clock hand swept around the circle to zero hour.

As if in an earthquake, the entire building rocked with the sound of the blast, as the explosive tore a hole into the vault door. Smoke and debris filled the room. Coughing and waving away the air in front of them, the four men climbed out from their individual shelters and approached the vault, and Dumos swung the door open.

The thieves stepped into the doorway, staring at their prize in awe. Three stacks of gold ingots, piled almost to eye-level, sat in the middle of the otherwise empty safe. Even in the darkness, they seemed to glisten. It was the kind of treasure men had fought for, killed and died for, all through history, and now it was theirs. They gazed at the gold in worshipful silence.

Dumos cleared his throat, bringing his men back to reality and the remaining tasks before them. One of the henchmen ran out of the room and came back a moment later, riding an electric forklift. As the forklift entered the vault, Dumos held a small two-way radio to his lips.

'We're coming out,' he said.

The three stacks of gold were piled upon a wooden pallet and the man on the forklift inserted its twin prongs underneath the platform. He pulled a lever, raising the pallet a few inches off the ground, and then, shifting the machine into reverse, he backed out of the vault.

George Scroope, bound and gagged, opened his eyes. He

was still groggy and it took him a second to focus. He saw the shadowy figures moving before him, and it seemed he could hear, in the distance, the sound of an approaching helicopter. When he saw the forklift loaded with gold rolling out of the vault, his mind immediately snapped to attention, clearing the cobwebs that clouded his vision. He knew he only had a moment or two in which to halt the robbery.

Flipping over on his back, George began to shimmy toward the wall. He slowly worked himself up along it until he reached a standing position. He was in the shadows, and since the gang were more interested in their loot than they were in him, none of them noticed as he hopped silently along the wall to the window.

Bracing himself, George rammed his shoulder into the window with all his strength. The glass shattered, and in that instant, the alarm went off, blaring resoundingly throughout the building.

Dumos' eyes flashed anger as he turned to this guard whose over-zealousness was threatening his schedule. He pulled out his Browning automatic and fired a quick burst at the man's chest.

George fell to the floor and lay very still.

SEVENTEEN

Ordinarily, the moment the alarm went off, a red light would have started flashing on Norman's computer console, alerting him to the trouble at the same instant as the police. But tonight there was no flashing light. As a matter of fact, nothing on the console was working quite the way it was supposed to.

'Jesse, what did you do?' Norman demanded in an accusing tone. The image on the closed-circuit video monitor was filling with static.

'Huh? What do you mean?' Jesse was already miles away from the Command Centre, heading for the test site. He didn't have the slightest idea what Norman was talking about.

'Did you do something to the bike? I'm losing you.'

'I didn't do anything,' Jesse replied defensively.

'Oh yeah? Well I don't think this is very fair. I mean, I know you didn't want to go out tonight, but to deliberately sabotage my motorcycle—'

'I didn't sabotage anything, Norman. What is going on?'

'I'm getting all this inter— oh no!' Norman cried as the video monitor went completely black. 'What happened now? Jesse, did you take off the helmet?'

'I couldn't hear you if I took off the helmet, could I?'

'No, I guess not,' Norman conceded. 'But I don't

understand it. I've completely lost my visuals.'

'I can tell you what you're missing,' Jesse said.

'I don't need a weather report. Jesse, you must have done something to the machine. This shouldn't be happening.'

Norman looked up at the vector map above his head. The red light that tracked Street Hawk's progress through the city streets was slowly fading out. Norman was aghast. His greatest nightmare was coming true; the computer was falling apart.

'Jesse, are you still there?' Norman asked, trying to hide the growing panic in his voice.

'Yeah, I'm still here. Norman, what's wrong?'

'You better bring Street Hawk back in.'

'But I'm almost at the test site.'

'Now, Jesse!' Norman shouted, losing his temper for one of the few times in his life. The other lights on the console in front of him were beginning to dim. Running his eyes over the panel, he desperately sought the source of the problem. He looked up at the vector map again, just in time to see it blink out. He tried manipulating dials and switches, to no effect. Slamming his fist down on the control panel, he slowly raised his eye to the map again, hoping that by some weird twist of fate, brute force had succeeded where technical expertise had failed. It hadn't. The lights on the console were gone.

'Jesse, are you coming in?'

'Yes, Norman. But I would like to remind you that if we'd done as I suggested and called off tonight's test, none of this would have happened.'

'Spare me the editorial comments and just bring the bike back in. And be careful on her, Jesse,' he added, sounding like a nagging wife. 'I can't afford for you to crack up the bike when I'm not in visual contact.'

'Hey, you know, just because you're having some problems on your end doesn't mean I've forgotten how to ride a motorcycle,' Jesse said as he slalomed around the traffic at breakneck speed. As long as Norman couldn't see him, he figured he might as well have some fun.

'Just be careful on her, okay?'

Jesse executed a hairpin turn around a corner. 'Sure, Norman, sure.'

If Jesse could have seen a few miles ahead of him, he would have known that extra caution was necessary. Because directly ahead of him, on the same route he was taking to get back to the warehouse, a war was about to break out.

Morton Street had once been the centre of a thriving business district. Suburban flight and brand-new shopping centres had eroded the financial base of the area, however, and urban decay had done the rest. Now, half the stores on the street stood abandoned, and the few that remained faced a daily struggle for survival.

The Savage Skulls had set up their headquarters in what used to be a very popular Chinese restaurant. Not too long ago, a typical evening would have seen the place jammed with families eating sweet and sour pork or chicken chow mein. No families came here now. The building's only visitors were members of a vicious gang whose major source of income was theft and whose major form of amusement was terrorizing nearby residents. The building was covered with graffiti, and the front window had been boarded up months ago. Above the door hung a huge unlit neon sign with the name 'Lee Chin' on it, a melancholy reminder of the building's happier past.

Phil Simpkins was parked across the street from the former restaurant. In the back seat were sitting Carl and Sally, and as Phil turned back to look at the teenager, he pointed across the way and asked, 'Is that where they took you, honey?'

The girl nodded.

Carl said, 'What are you going to do, Phil?'

'We're going to teach those punks a lesson, that's what we're going to do.'

'Nobody will get hurt, will they?' Carl asked, starting to wonder if he'd done the right thing coming to Phil.

'Of course someone will get hurt,' Phil replied, pointing at the Skulls' headquarters. 'They will. Now you just stay here with Sally. We'll take care of things from here on.'

Phil opened the door and climbed out. There were two

other cars parked behind his, and as Phil waved to them, their doors opened and eight men piled out. Like Phil, they all wore blue windbreakers that identified them as members of the Twelfth Street Protection Association. They carried baseball bats or tyre irons or other heavy objects, suitable for bashing in someone's head.

Phil removed his own baseball bat from his car and turned around to survey his troops. The men were all middle-aged and going to fat; their best years were definitely behind them. Even so, Phil figured they could handle a punk gang like the Savage Skulls.

Phil walked over to a garbage can on the sidewalk and began to strike it repeatedly with his baseball bat, trying to attract the attention of the men inside the building across the street. The other men followed his lead, and they too began hitting garbage cans or lamp posts with the objects they carried. A booming wallah of noise echoed through the street.

Phil raised his hand and the noise ceased. He stepped up to the curb and shouted at the building across the way. 'All right, you punks. The Twelfth Street Protection Association is cleaning up this neighbourhood and we don't want animals like you in it any more! So clear out of here!'

No reaction came from across the street; the building stood quiet.

'I said we want you out of here! Now either you're going to leave quietly, or we're going to have to go in there and drag you out! Which is it going to be?'

The front door swung ominously open and a single figure emerged, garbed in leather. He was Pug, the leader of the gang, a tall nineteen year old with a shaven head. Despite the lateness of the hour, he was wearing mirrored sunglasses.

'What are you fat pigs doing here in our neighbourhood?' Pug asked menacingly.

'This is our neighbourhood,' Phil replied. 'And tonight we're taking it back! So get yourselves in gear and clear out!'

'Come off it, old man. You don't have any right coming around here and giving us orders. We live here now. So why don't you just leave us alone and we'll leave you alone.'

'What about the girl you brought here this afternoon?

117

You weren't leaving her alone!'

Pug laughed. 'Her? She asked to come out here! She wanted to hang out with the Skulls.'

Carl jumped out of the car. 'You lying punk, you take that back!'

Phil turned on him. 'I said we'll take care of it!' he barked. 'Now get back in the car!'

Carl sullenly crawled back inside and closed the door behind him.

Phil turned back to the leader of the gang. 'You're lying, but it doesn't matter. We didn't come here to negotiate. We came here to clear you out.'

'Okay, old man, if that's the way you want it. But I warn you, we don't scare like those high school gangs you're used to. We fight for our turf.'

Pug snapped his fingers and the Savage Skulls began to file out of the building. They were a motley crew, eighteen and nineteen years old, wearing Savage Skull jackets and looking ready for action. They spread out in front of the building, fifteen of them in all.

Jesse was only a block away. As soon as he saw the two groups of men, each in their own distinctive uniforms, glaring at each other from opposite sides of the street, he braked to a halt. He surveyed the scene quickly and spotted Phil, standing at the forefront of his group of middle-aged warriors. Phil Simpkins could only mean one thing: trouble.

'Norman,' he said, 'I'm at the corner of Fifteenth and Morton. You better get the police out here right away.'

'What's going on?' Norman asked.

'It isn't break-dancing.'

Phil said, 'Let's get them.' The blue-jacketed army moved forward, waving their weapons in the air, ready to do battle.

Pug regarded them with a cocky grin on his face. 'Bad move, old man,' he said.

The Savage Skulls reached into their jackets and pulled out their own weapons. They didn't carry baseball bats or tyre irons. They carried switchblades and butcher knives and Pug and a few of the others standing beside him were

Pug protested as a police officer pulled him to his feet. 'We didn't do anything! Those guys attacked us and we were just defending ourselves! You don't have anything to arrest us on!'

The policeman pulled a switchblade out of Pug's jacket. 'Well, we can start with carrying a concealed weapon and go on from there, okay?'

Sally stepped out of the car and pointed at Pug. 'He hit me this afternoon. And those two—' she added, pointing at two other gang members, '—abducted me.'

Shoving Pug into one of the squad cars, the cops said, 'You see? We'll find plenty to hold you on.'

Phil shouted at them, 'And you creeps better watch it from now on. We don't want to see you hanging around here any more. Street Hawk is our boy, and if you show your faces in this neighbourhood again, he'll take care of you for good.'

Sam, the policeman, said, 'You just keep your big mouth shut, okay?'

Phil regarded him with total contempt. 'What if I don't? What are you going to do, arrest me?'

Sam opened the back door of the squad car. 'Yeah,' he said, pushing the vigilante inside.

By now, Jesse had reached the federal depository and as he saw the squad cars and ambulance parked out in front, he slowed down and said, 'Norman, there's been some trouble at the corner of Twenty-Sixth and Stratford. What happened?'

Norman looked up at the monitors on the control board, their blank faces mocking him like so many grinning gargoyles. 'I don't know,' he said sadly.

'You don't know?' What do you mean, you don't know?'

'Jesse, just bring the bike back. I'll explain when you get here.'

Jesse could tell by his tone of voice that it would be futile to question him further, so he turned the throttle and headed for home.

Usually, when Jesse neared the warehouse, the computer that monitored his progress opened the door for him. Jesse's reactions had become so automatic that he hardly paid any attention to it these days, and it wasn't until he reached the spot where he normally hit vertical lift that he looked up and saw the solid front of the billboard looming before him. He slammed on the airfoils, skidding to a halt only a few feet from the building.

'Norman,' he demanded, 'what the hell is going on? The billboard didn't open.'

Norman didn't seem surprised at all. 'Oh, that didn't work either? Just a minute, I'll open it manually.'

Jesse backed up and when the billboard opened, he resumed his approach into the warehouse. He landed inside and quickly dismounted, storming over to Norman with a peeved expression on his face.

'What is going on around here?'

Norman held up his hand. He was listening to the police radio. Jesse heard a voice crackling over the wire, saying, 'Reportedly escaped with an estimated one point two tons of gold.'

'What's that?' he asked.

'That's what you spotted at Twenty-Sixth and Stratford,' Norman explained. 'There was a gold robbery. They got away with over fifty bars.'

'That's worth millions!' Jesse exclaimed. 'How'd they do it?'

'Apparently, they escaped in a helicopter and a van.'

'Helicopter? That sounds like the same M.O. that group in Chicago was using a few months back.' Jesse noticed the control console for the first time. The ordinarily gleaming row of lights was completely dark. He looked at Norman. 'Norman, I was less than a mile away from there this evening. Why didn't your computer pick up the alarm?'

Norman became slightly evasive. 'Well, I've been having a few technical difficulties.' He wheeled over to the master control board and turned his back to Jesse.

'What kind of "technical difficulties"?' Jesse asked. 'Does it have anything to do with why it's so dark in here?'

'It's very technical and highly complicated. I'm afraid you wouldn't understand.'

122

Jesse shook his head. 'Oh no, Norman, you're not getting off that easy. Not after you told me that you were sure I had done something to hurt your pretty little machine. I want to know what's really wrong.'

Norman hesitated, eyeing Jesse uncertainly. He didn't want to tell him, but he knew Jesse would allow him no peace until he did.

'Well, to explain it in terms even you could understand . . . as you know, my system is interfaced with every major computer information bank and data program in the country, and they're all linked together by phone lines—'

'You didn't pay the phone bill?' Jesse asked.

Norman glowered at him. 'The phone company is replacing a group of underground lines. It doesn't affect normal service, but because everything in my system is interconnected, if you destroy one link, well. . .' He motioned to the dark console.

'So Street Hawk is shut down?' Jesse asked.

Norman nodded sadly.

'You're not considering suicide, are you?'

'It's only temporary,' Norman insisted. 'The phone company will finish their work on those lines as soon as possible.'

Jesse shook his head. 'Norman, they're the phone company. They don't have to.' He pulled down the zipper on his racing suit. 'But in the meantime, I guess I don't have any choice but to get on with my real life, huh?'

Norman sighed. 'I guess not,' he muttered.

EIGHTEEN

Every newspaper and television station in the city kept at least one reporter at police headquarters at all times. This really wasn't necessary; most days were pretty slow and the reporters spent a lot of time just sitting around waiting to be spoonfed press releases from the public relations department. But competition was so fierce between the various media that none of them dared risk not being there when an interesting story happened to develop.

This morning, the entire press corps was buzzing with excitement. Phil Simpkins had spent the night in jail for striking a police officer. The reporters relied on Simpkins a lot to spice up a slow news day, so today, when he had just cause for histrionics, they expected him to shine. They were hanging around the front of the station awaiting the arrival of Mary Simpkins, who was coming around to bail her father out.

'There she is!' one of the reporters cried as the attractive twenty year old brunette neared the building. The reporters pushed their way out the door, gathering around Mary like a pack of ravenous dogs.

'Why did your father do it?' a reporter asked.

'Is he guilty or is this a frame-up?' asked another.

Still a third reporter yelled out, 'How is Street Hawk

124

nvolved with your father?'

Mary waved her hand, trying to quieten down her inter-
rogators. She was accustomed to all the attention her father
had been getting since he started the Protection Association,
but she didn't have the flair for publicity he had.

'You'll have to ask my father all that,' she explained. 'I
don't have any answers for you.' She moved past the
disappointed reporters and went inside. The men and
women of the press followed her, to wait in the hallway for
Simpkins' release.

It took Mary thirty minutes to post bond and get her
father out of jail. When they were finally reunited, she gave
him a kiss and told him, 'There's a bunch of reporters out
here who want to have a talk with you.'

'Good,' Phil replied. 'I want to talk to them, too.'

He stepped out in the corridor, his daughter on his arm,
and the waiting members of the press surged forward and
shouted questions at him.

'Hold it, hold it!' he said, raising his hand. 'One at a
time.'

A fat man with a face like the man in the moon's cried
out, 'What happened last night? Did you really strike a
police officer?'

Phil shook his head. 'Of course not. I didn't hit him, I
accidentally bumped into him. The police are trying to
make it look like it was deliberate so they can keep me
behind bars.'

'Why?' asked the same reporter.

'Because we make them look bad. The police aren't doing
anything to stop crime in the streets. But we are. We're
showing that ordinary citizens are more capable of fighting
crime than the police are. The cops don't like it, so they
locked me up.'

A woman from one of the TV stations asked him, 'Is
Street Hawk involved with your organisation?'

Phil nodded. 'Absolutely. Street Hawk and the Protection
Association have the same goals: to protect the public from
all the goons and animals who are out there causing trouble.
When he heard about us he figured, hey, here's some guys

125

doing the same stuff I'm doing. I might as well help them out. So he joined up.'

'What can you tell us about Street Hawk?' shouted a bearded man at the back. 'Do you know who he really is?'

'Street Hawk and I made a deal. I don't talk about his private life, and he don't fix toilets.'

A wave of appreciative laughter swept through the corridor.

'What about last night, Phil?' another reporter asked. 'What were you doing over on Morton Street?'

'A very concerned father came to me last night,' Phil explained. 'It seems his daughter had been threatened by some punks who hang out on Morton Street. So me and the boys went over to have a talk with them and try to "convince" them to find a more hospitable neighbourhood. They didn't want to talk, they wanted to fight. So we fought. And we kicked their butts.'

'How would you respond to charges that your group is little more than an irresponsible vigilante organization?' asked a blonde woman in the front of the group.

Phil's face flushed with anger. He turned to the woman and, pointing his finger in her face, said, 'Let me tell you something about the word "vigilante". A vigilante is what you call somebody when he does something you don't like. If you like what he's doing, you call him a hero. When I went to Vietnam, I thought I was being a hero. When I came back, I found out that I'd been a vigilante. My country told me to go, and when I returned, I was told that doing what my country asked made me a criminal. Well, you know, I'm real proud of what I did in Vietnam. I went over there to fight for a lot of principles that I happen to think are kind of important. I went over there because I thought it would mean my daughter—' he put his arm around Mary's shoulder '—would grow up in a land that was safe and proud and free. But now it seems if we want our kids to grow up in that kind of country, we have another war to fight. And this one's in our own neighbourhoods, neighbourhoods all across America. It's a war against all the punks and the creeps and the animals that think they can push decent people around. And I promise you this: we may have lost in Vietnam, but we're going to win this war.'

There was a shocked silence for a moment, and then the moon-faced reporter started applauding. Someone else joined in, and in a moment, the whole crowd was applauding fervently. Phil swelled with pride.

Commander Altobelli happened to be walking down the hall in time to catch the tail end of Phil's speech. As soon as he heard his voice, he felt that familiar burning sensation in the pit of his stomach and tried to tiptoe away before anyone noticed him. Luck was not with him.

'Commander Altobelli,' the blonde reporter asked. 'Can you tell us the Police Department's position on Phil Simpkins and his organisation?'

Altobelli turned back to them. 'The Police Department's position is No Comment.'

Phil said, 'That's why this city is in such lousy shape. The only thing you can get out of them is "No comment". First you get "No comment" then you get no neighbourhoods.'

Another reporter yelled out, 'What about it, Commander? Are you also going to "No comment" us on the gold heist?'

'The press conference on the gold heist is scheduled for two pm,' Altobelli explained.

'You want a comment on the gold heist?' Phil asked. 'I can give you a comment on that.' The press corps turned back to him. 'While the cops were busy hassling a bunch of legitimate citizens who were just trying to protect themselves, that robbery was taking place less than a mile away. Right under the noses of the cops! Ain't that right, Commander?'

Several reporters swung their heads back toward Altobelli, but he said nothing.

'And let me tell you press guys something,' Phil continued, regaining their attention. 'All you guys want to talk about is the gold that was taken. Well, what about the guard who was shot? What do you know about him except that he's in the hospital? Well I happen to know a few things about him. His name is George Scroope. He lives a block and a half away from me. He's got two kids, a used car, and a dog with no pedigree. And he's a nice man. And you wanna know something else? He's me. And I'm him. That's what my "vigilante" organization is all about. People looking out for each other. Taking care of each other.'

While Phil held the reporters' attention, Altobelli snuck down the hall and ducked into the public relations office. Rachel was on the phone and Jesse was typing up a press release. Altobelli walked over to Jesse's electric typewriter and shut it off.

'What's wrong?' Jesse asked, looking up.

'That damn lunatic Simpkins is giving a press conference right down the hall from here. And he's making the department look like a bunch of idiots. I want you to shut him up.'

'How?' Jesse asked as he stood up.

'Shoot him,' Altobelli suggested. 'I don't care. Do whatever you have to do, just get that ape out of here.'

Jesse pleaded for help from Rachel, but she swung her chair around so she could pretend she didn't know anything about it. Sighing, Jesse stole out the door and Altobelli followed him. The police commander waited at the end of the corridor while Jesse crept silently down the hall toward the site of the impromptu press conference. Reaching a spot a short distance behind the reporters, Jesse paused to listen to Phil spout off for a moment, and then turned back to look at his boss.

Altobelli nodded, motioning with his hand that he wanted Jesse to do something. Jesse shrugged, holding his hands out with a confused look on his face as if asking what he should do. Altobelli waved his fist sternly, indicating that Jesse should act immediately. Jesse looked around and then, spotting the fire alarm on the wall beside him, he smashed it open, starting bells ringing through the entire building.

Altobelli winced, but the action seemed to have the desired effect. Phil stopped speaking, and the reporters looked around, confused. It took a second before a couple of them realized what the sound meant, and when they started moving toward the door, mumbling about the fire alarm, several others thought they must have actually seen the flame itself, and with cries of 'Fire! Fire!' the press corps stampeded toward the exit.

Jesse started back to his office, but Altobelli grabbed his arm. 'Talk to him, Mach. Now's the perfect opportunity.'

Rachel ran out of the office, yelling, 'There's a fire! Hurry! Hurry!' She rushed down the hall in a state of total panic. Jesse had to fight hard to keep from giggling as he and Altobelli turned around and followed her, pretending that they too believed the fire was real.

'I talked to him once already,' Jesse explained. 'He's not interested in helping us out.'

'I don't care what he is or isn't interested in,' Altobelli said as several more policemen ran past them. 'I want him to stop shooting his big fat mouth off. You can promise him whatever you want, but I don't want to see his ugly face on the front page any more. You got it?'

Jesse nodded. 'I'll talk to him.'

There was a big crowd standing in front of the station, waiting for the fire department to show up, and Jesse had trouble locating Phil amongst all these people. He finally spotted him from behind, walking down the street with his daughter. Jesse had to run to catch up with him.

'Mr Simpkins!' he called. Phil stopped and waited for Jesse to join him. 'Can I talk to you a second?'

Phil gave him the eye. 'So, Mach the cop, it's you again. What do you want this time? You want to talk about your Neighbourhood Watch Programme again?' he asked sarcastically.

'I'll go on ahead, Dad,' Mary said.

'I'll be right with you.' He turned to Jesse. 'Whatever you want, make it fast. I've got a friend to visit in the hospital.'

'George Scroope?' Jesse asked.

Phil nodded.

'He's going to be all right.'

'Yeah? How do you know?'

'I read the crime report this morning. His condition's serious, but stable. He'll pull through.'

'No thanks to the police,' Phil grumbled. He leaned against a car parked along the curb.

'You're right,' Jesse conceded. 'If we'd got there sooner,

George Scroope wouldn't be in the hospital today. The problem is, when crimes are committed, most of the time we don't know about it until it's too late. There's not enough of us to be everywhere in the city at once, so we have to rely on citizens to keep us informed when there's crime in the area.'

'And here comes the sales pitch,' Phil said, shaking his head. 'Look Mach, I've tried calling the police before. And you get a busy signal or the phone rings a dozen times and then you get put on hold. We can't count on the cops, not any more. If we see a problem, we'll take care of it ourselves.'

'And sooner or later, one of you is going to get hurt, the way George Scroope did last night,' Jesse pointed out. 'Look, we're willing to work with you, we'll train you in what to look for, we'll supply you with radios—'

'You want to help us? How about supplying us with some guns and some training in how to use them?'

'That's not going to happen and you know it,' Jesse said firmly.

'Then I don't think we got anything to talk about,' Phil replied. 'Call me if you got a better deal to offer, Mach. Or if you got problems with your plumbing. I'm in the Yellow Pages: Phil "The Flush" Simpkins. Now if you'll excuse me. I've got a friend to see.' He turned away and started to walk towards the hospital, just three blocks away.

Jesse called after him. 'Simpkins!' Phil looked back. 'I wanted to ask you something, just between you and me. That cop you "accidentally bumped into" last night . . . the story I heard was that he was about to shoot at Street Hawk. Any truth to that?'

'Just between you and me?' Phil asked. 'Yeah. Yeah, he was about to shoot at Street Hawk. And he missed. How about that?'

'I'm sure Street Hawk must be very grateful,' Jesse said quietly.

'Hey, he helps us out, we help him out. He's one of my boys, you know,' Phil bragged. 'And we take care of our own.'

NINETEEN

There were four fire trucks parked in front of the police station by the time Jesse got back. Several angry firemen were standing outside, waiting impatiently for the rest of their squad to return. As Jesse entered the building, he was passed by a few others, grumbling and complaining as they walked back out to their truck.

In the hallway, Altobelli was getting dressed down by the local fire captain. 'If there's one place I wouldn't expect a false alarm, it would be here. That's the sort of thing you get at high schools.'

Altobelli explained, 'Hey, you know, we get all sorts of creeps around here. It was probably some guy brought in on a misdemeanour charge or something like that.'

Jesse covered his mouth with his hand to hide his laughter as he walked nonchalantly toward the two men. Altobelli's eyes shot daggers at him as he passed and he slipped quietly back into his own office, where he was surprised to find Rachel standing at his desk and talking on his phone.

'Oh yes, that's wonderful,' she was saying as he walked in the door. 'We'll see you then. Oh, and Jesse just came in. I'll put him on.'

She handed the phone to Jesse. 'It's Deborah Shain. She's going to do the spot for us. I owe you one, Jesse.'

131

Jesse smiled and took the phone. Rachel walked over to the file cabinet and opened a drawer, looking for her file on Deborah Shain.

'Hi, Deborah,' Jesse said.

'Hi. I just told Rachel I want to shoot the anti-drug spot for the Police Department. And Artie wants to do it with me!'

'That's great. I guess you changed your mind about cops, huh? I told you they were on your side.'

'Yeah, well I guess cops really aren't that bad,' she admitted. 'But you know, it wasn't the police that saved me, not really. It was Street Hawk.'

'Oh. Well, how do you know Street Hawk isn't a cop in real life?'

Deborah laughed. 'Are you kidding? That guy's too cool. I wouldn't believe that for a second.'

'You're right,' Jesse said, laughing. 'Neither would I. Say Deborah, I was wondering, now that you've decided you don't hate every cop in the world, maybe you wouldn't mind going out with me on Saturday.'

Rachel removed the file from the drawer. She turned around and gave Jesse a curious glance, but he waved her away. Slamming the drawer shut, she went back to her desk and pouted.

Deborah said, 'Well, we're shooting the commercial on Saturday—'

'Oh.' Jesse tried to prevent the disappointment from showing in his voice.

'—but I'm free in the evening!'

'Hey, that's great! I could pick you up right after the shoot and we could go out to dinner or something.'

Deborah giggled. 'Yeah. I might be real interested in that "or something".'

Jesse grinned. 'I'll see you then.'

'Right,' Deborah answered.

He hung up. Rachel shot up from her desk and quickly circled Jesse, a knowing look on her face. 'Is she going out with you?' she teased.

Jesse nodded, still grinning. 'She sure is.'

'I guess you would have never met her if I hadn't asked

you to see her for me, huh?'

Jesse shrugged. 'No, come to think of it, I guess not.'

'Jesse, remember when I said I owed you one?'

'Yeah.'

'It's cancelled.'

The first thing Phil Simpkins saw when he got off the elevator on the fourth floor of City Hospital was his daughter, talking to a group of men sitting in the lobby. The men were there for the same purpose he was and Phil knew every one of them; they had all been with him the night before.

Mary approached her father. 'It's okay, Dad. Mr Scroope is going to be all right.'

'I heard. I just wanted to come by and see for myself how he was getting along.'

A couple of the men stood up and walked over to Phil. Joey Rodriguez, an overweight mechanic who was rarely seen without a candy bar in his hand, slapped Phil on the shoulder affectionately, getting chocolate stains on his shirt. 'I'm sorry they took you in last night, Phil,' he said.

'Eh, it's no big deal,' Phil said. 'The cops thought a night in jail would cool me off.'

Mary laughed. 'It sounded to me like it only made you hotter.'

The rest of the men laughed too.

'Was it rough in there, in jail?' asked Abe Weinstein, a short grey-haired cab driver.

Phil shook his head. 'Not for me, it wasn't. Those punks had too much sense to mess with me.' He spotted George's wife, Cathy, stepping out of a room halfway down the hall, and he said, 'Excuse me a minute.'

Wiping the chocolate off his shoulder, Phil walked down the hall towards Cathy. She had always been a pretty woman, but now it looked like she had aged twenty years overnight. Her face was etched with pain and her eyes were red from all the crying she'd been doing. Phil put his arms around her and embraced her. He could feel the trembling, the fear, the sadness, as she nestled against him, and he slowly released her.

'I heard the good news,' he said. 'He's going to be all right, huh?'

She nodded. 'That's what the doctor says. But I don't know if you can ever be all right after something like that. I know I won't. All those years he's been working there, I've never had to worry, not once. He used to say, "Who's going to wanna steal from the government? They don't have any money." We used to laugh about it, how safe he was. But if he goes back to that job, from now on, every time he goes to work, I'll be wondering if he'll ever come home again.'

Phil felt helpless and frustrated. He didn't know what to say or how to reassure her. Instead, he asked, 'May I see him?'

'Just for a minute. He's sleeping.' She crept into George's room and Phil followed silently behind her. They stood in the door, gazing at the sleeping man. George was lying under an oxygen tent and the clear plastic shelter expanded and contracted with every breath he took. Even in sleep, George seemed to be racked with pain.

'The bullet pierced his lung,' Cathy explained.

Phil nodded. He balled his hands into fists and squeezed tightly, trying to fight the rage inside him. He wanted to punch somebody. Yesterday, George had been healthy, robust, smiling. And today he needed a machine's help in order to breathe. It just wasn't fair.

Cathy motioned to Phil and the two of them stepped back out in the hallway. He put his arm around her and embraced her again gently.

'You need anything, Cathy? You fixed okay for cash?'

'George's boss said he'll keep him on salary until he can get out of here.'

'That's good.' He stepped back and looked at her. 'But you look tired. You should get some rest.' Phil called his daughter over. 'Mary, take Mrs Scroope home. And tell your Mom to cook something up for her and the kids tonight. We'll send it over later.'

'She's making some chicken for them right now, Dad,' Mary explained.

Cathy's eyes welled with tears. 'Oh, thank you, Phil. But

you don't have to do anything for me. Really. The kids and me, we can take care of ourselves.'

'Yeah, but you don't have to,' the plumber responded. 'You got friends.'

Mary put her arm around Cathy's shoulder and led her to the elevator. The men in the hallway stood up respectfully as the wounded man's wife walked past them. Just as she reached the elevator, Cathy turned around, her eyes alive with pain and danger. 'Why did he do it, Phil? All he had to do was just lie there! If he hadn't sent in that alarm, he'd be okay now!'

'It was his job,' Phil responded. 'He did what he had to do.'

'Why does everybody have to be a hero? Why does anybody have to be a hero?' She swept her hand in front of her, indicating Phil and all the other men in the corridor. 'What are you men doing, going out every night and getting in fights? You have families and businesses to take care of! Isn't that enough?'

The men looked away or at the floor. Only Phil had the courage to meet Mrs Scroope's accusing eyes.

Mary said quietly, 'My father just wants things to be the way they were when I was a little girl.'

'Those days are gone,' Cathy said. She started to cry. 'You know, the worst thing about it is, the police don't even know who they're looking for. They got away scot-free. What George did was a waste, a total waste.'

The elevator door opened and Mary led the weeping woman over to it. 'Come on, Mrs Scroope. We're going home now.' They stepped in and the elevator door closed. The hallway was filled with an embarassed silence. Cathy Scroope's last words hung in the air long after she was gone.

'She's right,' Phil said. 'The cops will never find those guys. If we want to stop them, we'll have to do it ourselves.'

'You're crazy,' Abe said. 'Those guys are out of our league.'

Joey said, 'Let the police handle the gold robbers. We'll just take care of the neighbourhood.'

'This is part of the neighbourhood,' Phil pointed out.

'Who knows who they'll shoot next time? If we're really serious about protecting people's lives, this gang is just as dangerous as any of the other ones we've tangled with.'

Abe said, 'But we don't know anything about fighting big-time crooks like this. We don't know who they are, where they're going to strike next—'

'Abe, how many cab drivers we got in the neighbourhood?'

Abe shrugged. 'I don't know. Ten, twelve maybe.'

'And truck drivers?'

'About the same,' Abe answered.

'And we got longshoremen, dispatchers, maintenance men . . . we got a better network of information than the cops do. If everybody just pulls together and helps on this thing, we can find those crooks. And stop them.'

Joey said, 'I don't know. It could be dangerous.'

'Not as dangerous as letting a bunch of punk hoods think they can get away with shooting decent men like George.' Phil was getting excited now. 'Listen, this isn't just about a bunch of gold robberies. This is about who runs our neighbourhoods, the folks that live in them or some hoods who think having a gun makes them tough. This is as much what we've been fighting for as anything, and I ain't gonna turn away from it, just cause these bums got a better rep than some of the other guys we've taken on.'

The other men looked at Phil. His enthusiasm was infectious.

'I'm with you, Phil,' Joey said.

'So am I,' said one of the others. The rest of the men chimed in their agreement.

'Good. We're all in it, right?'

The men nodded.

Phil grinned. 'Those gold robbers ain't got a chance.'

TWENTY

Phil didn't have time to prepare for his search for the gold hijackers that evening. There was a lot of work to be done still and a lot of information was required before he could set up a sensible plan of attack. The word spread through the neighbourhood of Phil's intentions and his phone rang off the hook with people calling to find out how they could help.

The plumber wasn't the only one who was interested in catching those gold robbers, however. Jesse had done some research at police headquaters and, despite his protestations of the night before, he'd decided that Street Hawk was needed tonight. As soon as he got off work, he headed for the Command Centre.

Norman was on the phone when Jesse got there.

'May I talk to a person, please?' he heard him saying. Jesse stared at the engineer in astonishment. He looked bleary-eyed and dishevelled, more like a mad scientist from an old horror film than the level-headed technician Jesse knew. He paced back and forth, shouting into the phone. 'I don't want to call another number!' Norman screamed. 'I want to talk to a human being! Right now!' Norman paused, listening to the response on the other end. 'Okay, cut with the music already! Just put a person on! Hello? Hello?' He slammed down the receiver, seething with frustration.

'Norman, what are you doing?' Jesse asked calmly.

'I am trying to get in touch with somebody at the phone company who can tell me when the lines will be repaired. But all I get are these recorded messages telling me what a great job the phone company's doing and giving me another number to call for more information. And when I call that number, I get still another recording. I tell you, I'm not sure there's any people at all at the phone company. I think the whole place is run by a bunch of tape players.'

Jesse was stunned. 'You were talking to a recording?'

'I had to! There's no one else to talk to!'

Jesse shook his head. It sounded to him like Norman was going over the deep end, but he decided not to press it. 'I was kind of hoping you'd be operational by now. Street Hawk has to go out tonight.'

'Absolutely not. There's no way I'm putting my bike out on the street without my computers in full operation.'

'Norman, I have to go out. I've been looking into this gold robbery we missed last night. If it's the same group that was operating in Chicago a while back, they're going to strike again tonight. That's the way they did it in Chicago. They struck every night in a row until the shipping companies started to panic and refused to ship the gold. Then they disappeared from sight.' Jesse showed Norman the stack of papers he was carrying in his hand. 'Look at this. I got these printouts from the Police Department computers. There's four truck depots in town that are storing gold tonight.'

Norman took the papers and studied them. 'I wish I had my own printouts,' he muttered.

'These will do fine,' Jesse said. 'It's the same information.'

Norman remained hesitant. 'It's dangerous for you to go out by yourself. There's no hyperthrust.'

'So what? I can still ride. Just because a couple of phone wires are down doesn't mean the whole system falls apart.'

'It's more like two thousand, eight hundred and sixty pairs of wires, all carefully integrated and cross-connected.'

'Okay,' Jesse acknowledged, 'so it's more than a couple. That still doesn't mean I can't go out.'

'I thought you didn't want to go out. You said you

wanted to go on with your own life.'

'That's before I realized what those gold thieves were up to. Come on, Norman, it's a perfect case for Street Hawk.'

Norman was not convinced. 'I don't know. . .'

Jesse pointed at the darkened console. 'You have more faith in that pile of nuts and bolts than you do in me, don't you?'

'Well, it's usually more reliable—'

'Not tonight it isn't! Look Norman, you can't count on machines to do everything for you, no matter how complicated or sophisticated they are. Sometimes you have to count on people, too.'

'Well. . .' He looked at the printouts. 'I guess it might work. But I want you to stay in constant contact with me, so I always know where you are.' Norman looked up, but Jesse was already on his way to the change room to suit up. 'And don't take any foolish risks with the bike!'

Jesse turned round and grinned. 'Hey, I never do, do I?'

'Jesse, what are you singing?' Norman demanded.

It was near dawn and he and Jesse were both exhausted. Jesse had been patrolling all night, riding from warehouse to warehouse, hoping for some sign of the criminals. There hadn't been any.

'It's called "Golden Eyes",' Jesse explained. 'It's a Deborah Shain tune. You like it?' Jesse sang louder. ' "He's got golden eyes, he's—" '

'I despise it,' Norman said, cutting him off. 'Just tell me where you are.'

Jesse was outside the chain link fence that circled the perimeter of one of the truck depots. He looked up at the sign over the front gate and read it aloud to Norman. 'Citywide Warehouse and Storage. Third time I've been here tonight. And all is quiet.'

Several mammoth trucks bearing the Citywide logo were parked outside the largest of the warehouses, but the only person in sight was the youthful guard at the front gate, reading a newspaper. As Jesse rode past him, the guard looked up and, recognizing Street Hawk and not considering his presence a matter of concern, went back to his reading.

The black sky was beginning to grey as the sun peeked over the horizon and a soft thin mist hung in the air. A few early rising birds were singing in the nearby trees, trying to awaken their friends and cousins. It did not appear to be the sort of setting in which a robbery was imminent.

'Maybe you were wrong about there being another robbery tonight,' Norman suggested.

'Maybe I was,' Jesse admitted. 'I'll patrol for another hour or so, untill it gets light. Then I'll head in.'

Jesse turned onto the main road and sped off toward the next trucking depot on his list. On his way up the road, he passed a black van with the Citywide logo painted on the side. It was a little early for work, but in the trucking business, Jesse figured, a lot of people worked a twenty-four hour day.

The black van pulled up to the front gate. With a furrowed brow, the security guard looked up from his paper and scratched his head. He wasn't expecting anybody at this hour. He set down his newspaper and stepped outside to see what was going on.

'How you doin'?' he greeted as he walked over to the driver. He froze. The driver was wearing a nylon stocking over his face and a similarly-garbed man sat in the passenger seat, pointing a Uzi machine gun straight at him.

'Hands up,' the driver said. The guard raised his hands.

The rear door of the van sprang open and another Uzi-armed gunman jumped out. He pushed the guard back into the shed and nodded at the front gate. 'Open it,' he ordered.

The guard raised the gate and the van rolled through. It drove toward the main warehouse and stopped at the bottom of a ramp that led to a huge steel overhead door. Albert, behind the wheel, gunned the engine impatiently.

The gunman held the barrel of the machine gun against the guard's neck. 'Call inside. Tell them you just got in a delivery and have them open the door.'

The guard swallowed nervously. He picked up the phone and dialled the number for the inside of the warehouse.

'Try anything funny,' the gunman warned him, 'and even your own widow won't be able to identify you.'

The guard nodded. He said, 'We got a delivery. Open the door.'

There were two guards inside the warehouse. The one on the phone looked at the shipping manifold hanging next to the door. 'There's no shipments on here for this morning,' he pointed out.

'Yeah, I know,' the man outside assured him. 'Paperwork's messed up again.'

'Okay.' The guard hung up the phone and turned to his partner. 'They got a delivery this morning. Do you believe that?'

The other man shook his head. 'They don't tell us anything around here.'

The first guard hit a button next to the warehouse door and it started to rise.

At the front gate, the gunman knocked his prisoner over the head with the butt of the machine gun and the guard fell to the floor. His assailant walked toward the warehouse to join his companions.

As soon as the overhead door was high enough, Albert put the van in gear and pushed the accelerator down to the floorboards. The van screeched into the warehouse and the two guards, caught by surprise, scampered out of the way. With a bang, the van door shot open and three more masked men, all armed with submachine guns, jumped out and pointed their weapons at their helpless prisoners. The guards raised their hands.

'Should we tie them up?' one of the henchmen asked.

Albert climbed out of the van. He gazed at the two trembling men and then turned his attention to the far end of the room, where three stacks of gold bars lay shimmering on a wooden pallet. 'I don't want anyone sending in any premature alarms,' he said.

The two guards were certain they were dead men, and they silently mouthed their prayers as Albert approached them. The masked man shoved a chloroform-covered handkerchief over each of the men's mouths and noses, and they fell to the floor, unconcious. 'All right, let's get to work,' Albert said.

'The boss would have shot them,' one of the other

gunmen suggested.

'I didn't think it was necessary,' Albert replied. He admired Dumos' careful planning but he did not appreciate his often uncalled-for ruthlessness. He pulled out a small two-way radio and spoke into it.

'We're inside. We'll have the gold out in a few minutes.'

Dumos' voice came over the speaker. 'Excellent,' he said. 'We'll be there shortly.'

Dumos was sitting in the helicopter on top of an office building a few miles away. Shutting off the radio, he turned to the pilot and said, 'Let's go.'

The pilot started up the whirlybird and the propeller rapidly picked up speed. In a moment, the vehicle was airborne and they were heading in the direction of Citywide Warehouse and Storage.

It was a few minutes later when Jesse spotted the 'copter. He was going east, the helicopter was going west. Jesse stopped and watched as it flew directly overhead and past him. He turned the bike around and continued to watch it growing smaller in the distance.

'Norman, can you get Air Traffic?' he asked.

Norman looked at the radio lying on top of the computer console. 'No. I get Police, Fire, Weather, and Citizen's Band. But no Air Traffic. What's up?'

'A Bell Ranger, westbound at about six hundred feet. And there're no markings on it.'

'That's awful low,' Norman pointed out. 'You think maybe it's a police 'copter?'

'With a hoisting rig tucked under its belly? No, I think this might be our boys, Norman.'

He kicked the bike into gear and tore after the helicopter. It was difficult to keep up; the chopper was already several blocks ahead of him, and Jesse was forced to keep one eye in the air and the other one on the road in front of him.

'Norman, he's getting away,' Jesse said. 'Can you give me hyperthrust?'

'Not without the computers,' Norman replied. 'You'll end up splattered against the side of a building.'

'Forget it.'

'I already did. Be careful, Jesse.'

'I will,' Jesse said.

The Bell Ranger was pulling ahead of him. Jesse increased his speed and whizzed through a red light. A car going the other way slammed on its brakes, and Jesse skimmed around it. He heard the driver screaming behind him and felt sweat pour down his forehead. This was not the way he liked to travel.

The helicopter drifted off to the right and Jesse turned down an alley, trying to take a short cut. There was a brown wooden fence at the end of the alley and Jesse hit vertical lift and flew over it. A cat shrieked in utter terror as he thumped to the ground on the other side of the fence and continued the chase.

Dumos had not yet noticed his pursuer but from his perch high in the air he could see the yard at Citywide Storage. A forklift was setting the precious bundle of gold down in the centre of the yard a little distance from where Albert had parked the van, and two of his henchmen looked up at the 'copter and waved.

'There!' Dumos cried, pointing at them.

'I see them,' the pilot said as he descended into the yard. He flew low, bringing the machine over the stack of gold and stopping there, hovering in the air. He lowered the thick iron grappling hook on the hoisting mechanism. On the ground below, the two henchmen grabbed it and tucked it carefully beneath a set of steel bars that wound around their newly won treasure.

As Jesse neared the warehouse, he could see the theft in progress through the chain link fence. 'Norman, we struck gold,' he said. 'Get the police to Citywide Storage now!'

Waiting for Albert to assure him the hoist was secure, Dumos' eyes wandered over the yard. He spotted Street Hawk pulling to a stop outside the chain link fence and muttered, half to the pilot and half to himself, 'We could have trouble.'

Albert tugged on the hoist and, seeing that everything was fastened tightly, he moved out in front of the 'copter and signalled to Dumos that all was well. 'Let's go!' Dumos shouted. 'Now!'

The 'copter started to ascend, pulling the precious bundle up below it.

Jesse hit the particle beam and fired it at the fence. Bright red sparks shot off the metal as the chain dissolved and a section of the fence crashed to the ground. Jesse burst into the yard like a torpedo.

Dumos had his own Uzi inside the helicopter and, as soon as Jesse flew into the yard, he picked it up and fired a few rounds in his direction. The henchmen, whose eyes had been raised upward watching the helicopter's departure, followed the direction of the gunfire and spotting Street Hawk for the first time, started firing their own weapons at him.

Jesse shot behind a building as the bullets rained past him. He circled the structure, coming up on the criminals from behind. Guns screaming, he bore down on the villains and forced them to turn tail and run, ducking behind the van for safety.

'Turn! Turn!' Dumos screamed as he pointed at Jesse. The 'copter tilted as the pilot twisted it around, trying to put the motorcycle within firing range.

Jesse looked up and locked the targeting system on the hoisting mechanism. He fired the laser. In a bright orange flash of light, the grappling hook shattered and the gold fell back to earth. The yard shook as more than a ton of the precious metal struck the ground.

Dumos howled. 'Get him!'

Freed of its heavy burden, the chopper looped around and dived at Street Hawk from the rear. Dumos leaned out the door and fired round after round of machine gun fire at him.

With no time to dodge or manoeuvre, Jesse gunned the bike forward, just ahead of the pursuing 'copter. As he flew past the van, he fired a burst from his own guns. The bullets hammered into the ground, forcing Albert and the others to duck underneath the vehicle. Jesse flew up the ramp through the open warehouse door and the helicopter veered upwards and away.

Jesse deployed the air foils, coming to an instant halt. He swivelled the bike around and started toward the door again.

Albert climbed out from beneath the van and fired a few short bursts from his Uzi at the top of the overhead door. A couple of bullets tore open the braking system and the door crashed downward, just as Jesse was speeding toward it. He screeched to a standstill as the heavy steel door struck the ground with an ear-bursting clap.

In the distance, Albert could hear the sound of approaching police sirens. 'We're getting out of here,' he shouted. His men quickly climbed back in the van and Albert jumped behind the wheel. The van took off, shooting through the front gate.

In the circling helicopter overhead, Dumos too could hear the sound of police sirens. Fuming and cursing, he instructed the pilot to head out of there. The helicopter flew off to safety as Dumos kept his eyes on the treasure he was forced to leave behind. Already, he was making plans to get revenge on Street Hawk.

Inside the warehouse, Jesse hit the button next to the door, but nothing happened. He pounded it several times in frustration.

'Norman,' he said, 'they got away. And I'm trapped inside the warehouse.'

Norman said, 'You've got to get out of there fast. The police should be there any minute.'

Jesse heard the sounds of the police cars pulling up outside the warehouse. 'They're already here,' he said. He looked around for another door, but there didn't seem to be one. The two guards lay unconscious on the floor, not too far away, and Jesse jumped off the bike and ran over to them. He tried to awaken them, but they were dead to the world.

Outside, the police officers started pounding on the heavy steel door. Jesse looked at it and, for the first time, noticed the early morning rays of sunlight filtering through the huge transom window above the door. Raising his eyes to the window, he thought for a moment and then looked back to the bike, trying to gauge their relative sizes.

'Jesse, where are you?' Norman shouted frantically. 'Are you still in the warehouse?'

'Not for long,' Jesse assured him. He climbed back on

Street Hawk, kicked the starter, and darted across the warehouse to the far wall. Spinning around, he looked across the cavernous room, estimating the distance to the door and the height of the window. He'd have to get this one just right or else they'd be scraping him off the wall.

He gunned Street Hawk forward, flying across the room at the solid steel door. He hit vertical lift and the bike shot into the air, crashing through the window.

Outside, the policemen stared in awe as Jesse sailed over them and hit the ground on the far side of the police cars. They watched helplessly as he sped off toward the gate and freedom.

TWENTY-ONE

'Well?' Altobelli demanded.

Jesse looked up at him, confused. He'd only arrived at the office about two minutes ago and already Altobelli was hovering over his desk, glaring at him as if Jesse had just rear-ended his car.

'Well, what?' he asked.

Altobelli turned to Rachel. 'What is with this guy? Doesn't he ever read the papers?'

'Give me a break,' Jesse pleaded. 'I was running late this morning. I barely had time to shave.'

Rachel walked over to his desk, a folded-up newspaper in her hand. She showed Jesse the headline: 'Vigilante Group Claims "If Cops Can't, We Will" ' and started to read the article aloud. 'Phil Simpkins, the pugilistic plumber, claims that he and Street Hawk can and will flush out the gold hijackers who have been—'

'Spare me,' Altobelli pleaded. 'It's committed to memory.' He turned to Jesse. 'I thought you were going to keep that plumber's mouth shut.'

'I've tried, Commander. I've talked to him twice now. It doesn't seem to do any good.'

'Well, talk to him again!' Altobelli demanded. 'Do you know how many ulcers I've got?'

Jesse sighed.

'Look, Mach, all kidding aside, when guys like Simpkins make the department look bad, it makes it a lot more difficult for us to do our job. Like those gold robberies. You know, I wanted to put extra officers on to guard the truck depots and gold depositories at night. I started calling these guys to talk about security and they didn't even want to talk to me. They said they didn't trust the police and they didn't think we knew what we're doing. So last night, there's another gold robbery, and we're not anywhere near the place. The only one who even gets close to those crooks is Street Hawk, and even he's working for Simpkins, now.'

'I'm not so sure about that,' Jesse said.

'What?'

'That Street Hawk's working for Simpkins. But I guess that's not the point, is it? The point is somebody's got to shut Simpkins up.' He smiled at Rachel. 'Interested?'

She shook her head. 'I think this one's more your kind of mission.'

'I had a feeling you'd say that.' He stood up. 'So I'll talk to him. But you know, if I don't have anything solid to offer, I can't very well expect him to do what we ask.'

'Offer him anything you like. Just get him out of the papers.'

'How about dropping the charges against him?'

Altobelli turned beet-red. 'I can't do that! The man struck a police officer!'

Jesse said, 'The way I understand it, you had a trigger-happy cop who was about to shoot Street Hawk in the back. Now maybe what Phil did was illegal, but it's lucky he did it. What do you think would have happened if he hadn't done anything and the cop actually did shoot Street Hawk? I can see the headlines now: "Street Hawk Stops Riot, So Police Kill Him".'

'All right, Mach, you've made your point. I'll arrange to have the charges dropped.'

'Good,' Jesse said. 'And I'll see what I can do to keep Phil quiet.'

'I'm sure you can do it, Jesse,' Rachel interjected. 'I have great faith in you. When you turn on the charm, not very many people can resist.'

'I don't think I can handle Simpkins quite the same way I handled Deborah Shain.'

'Oh,' Rachel teased, 'you're not going to ask him out for a date? I think you can talk him into it anyway.'

Jesse looked at Rachel, a bit surprised. 'Why all these words of encouragement?'

'Because if you get Simpkins to quiet down, maybe he—' she said, pointing at Altobelli '—will stop talking about his ulcers!'

Jesse laughed. 'No chance.'

'Very funny,' Altobelli responded. 'Just take care of it, Mach.' He started for the door, then turned back to Jesse. 'And try not to involve the fire department this time, okay?'

There was a small crowd of people milling around the front of Phil Simpkins' shop. Some of them were members of the Association, but for the most part, the men and women standing out in front were mere curiosity seekers, attracted by all the headlines Phil had garnered recently and by the way he'd decorated his shop. Instead of the plumbing fixtures that normally occupied the window, there now hung a big banner proclaiming this the headquarters of the Twelfth Street Protection Association, 'fighting for law, order, and safe neighbourhoods'. Beneath this was displayed an American flag, Phil's war medals, and a bulletin board full of headlines and newspaper articles recounting the Association's latest deeds. The shop looked more like a political headquarters than a place of business.

Jesse drove slowly down the street, looking for a place to park. There wasn't a space to be had and Jesse couldn't help but notice that more than one of the cars on the street bore the bald eagle logo that designated them as 'official' vehicles of the Association. As he reached the corner where Phil's shop stood, he pulled to a stop and shook his head at all the activity. Phil had certainly become popular quickly. Two men stepped out of the shop, both wearing the familiar blue windbreakers and carrying truncheons. They looked more like Little League fathers than guardians of the city, but they walked straight and tall with a determined glint in their eyes, men with a mission. Crossing the street, they climbed into one of the 'official' vehicles. They pulled away from the curb and Jesse quickly did a U-turn and grabbed their parking space.

Jesse approached the front door of the shop. The people on the sidewalk stepped aside, clearing a path for him. As Jesse moved toward the door, he distinctly heard the words, 'Cop' and 'Policeman' whispered from ear to ear. Feeling like the carrier of a rare and infectious disease, Jesse opened the door of the shop and stepped inside. He flirted with the idea of wiping the doorknob with his handkerchief, but decided that might be carrying things a little too far.

Phil had turned the plumbing shop into his very own Command Centre. Hanging on the wall was a map of the neighbourhood and next to it was a chart indicating who was in charge of patrolling which blocks and at what hours. Phil's desk was covered with mimeographed sheets, and Jesse could read on one of them, 'In case of trouble, call Phil Simpkins at. . . ' Mary was in the corner, running off more pages on the mimeograph machine. Pipes and fixtures and tools were strewn all over the floor and workbench, and Jesse had to step around this chaos to get to Phil's desk.

There were two men in their forties, new recruits, standing in front of the desk waiting for Phil to give them further instructions. Phil was on the phone, his florid face framed by the toilet seat display behind him, and as he spoke, he looked at his daily schedule on his desk calendar. 'Okay, why don't you come in around two o'clock,' he said, 'and we'll see if we can get you started. . . Good, I'll see you then.'

He hung up and grinned at the two men. 'Another volunteer,' he explained. 'Now, as I was saying, if you run into something you can't handle, you give us a call on CB Channel Six. Or if the cops start hassling you.' He gave Jesse a dirty look, acknowledging his presence for the first time. 'I'm used to dealing with cops.'

He handed the two men mimeographed sheets. 'Read over this list of instructions before you go out tonight, and if you have any questions, gimme a call. Or talk to Mary here,' he added, nodding to his daughter. 'She should be able to help you.'

'Thanks, Phil,' the first man said.

'I have a question,' said the other man eagerly. 'When do we get the jackets?'

'Give Mary ten bucks and tell her your size, and she'll order one for you.'

The man nodded. 'I'll bring the money tomorrow, Mary.'

She smiled condescendingly.

The men left the shop. Jesse looked around, saying, 'It's quite an operation you got here.'

'Yeah,' Phil acknowledged. 'And it's partly thanks to you guys. Since you threw me in jail, I've had more volunteers than I know what to do with.'

Jesse said, 'Well, I hope it doesn't spoil things for you, but we're dropping the charges.'

Phil was surprised. 'You are? Why?'

'I had a little talk with the Commander this morning. I convinced him that people shouldn't have to go to jail for keeping a trigger-happy cop from making a dumn mistake.'

'Thanks, Mach. You're all right.'

'Now that I've done a favour for you, maybe you can do one for me.'

'Oh boy,' Phil responded sarcastically. 'More talk.'

'No,' Jesse said, 'what I want is less talk. From you. You've been making a lot of noise lately and making it very difficult for people in the Police Department to do their jobs. And we're getting tired of it.'

Phil rose to his feet and stepped out from behind the desk. 'Mary, would you go outside for a minute?'

Mary looked concerned. Her eyes darted from her father to Jesse and back again, but she did as her father told her. She knew better than to disagree with him when his blood was boiling, as it was doing now.

As she walked out the door, Phil looked out the window and saw his friends and neighbours outside, their faces pressed against the glass, waiting for something to happen. He knew they were counting on him as defender of the faith

151

and he didn't mean to let them down. He turned to Jesse

'So you're sick of it, huh?' he prodded. 'What are you going to do about it?'

'Listen, Simpkins,' Jesse said, pointing his finger at him, 'this is no joke. It's real easy for people on the outside to criticize us, because you can just talk out of total ignorance and don't have to worry about the facts. You don't think the police care about crime in the streets. Well, let me tell you something. We do care. We care a great deal. But we're understaffed, we're underpaid, and we never know when some nut out there's going to take a potshot at us. We do the best we can with our limited resources. But when some egotistical clown like you comes along making unfounded accusations against us for the sake of a few headlines, it makes it ten times more difficult for us to do our jobs. So why don't you just put a lock on it?'

'You can't talk to me like that!' Phil snarled.

'Oh yeah? I just did!'

Glaring at him, Phil roared angrily and moved forward, swinging his massive fist at Jesse's mouth.

Jesse pulled his head back, letting the fist sail past him. Phil followed with another punch, from his left this time, and again Jesse ducked aside.

'This isn't going to accomplish anything, Phil,' Jesse said, trying to calm down his opponent. 'And someone could get hurt.'

Phil growled, charging at him like a mad bull, and Jesse quickly moved out of the way. Phil fell over his workbench and his tools clattered all over the floor.

'Not to mention the damage to the furniture,' Jesse added.

Phil got up, breathing hard and heart pounding. His face a mask of sweat, he charged again, with hands outstretched in a murderous rage, as if he intended to strangle him. Again, Jesse eluded his attack and Phil slammed into the wall behind his desk, knocking loose the toilet seat display. Phil covered his head with his arms as the seat covers rained down on him.

Jesse sighed. 'You done?'

Phil turned around, his face steaming as he tried to catch his breath. 'Just hang on a minute till I get my breath back.'

Jesse's mouth dropped open. 'What are you, crazy?'

Phil paused, letting the stupidity of what he had just said sink in. He started to laugh. 'Yeah, I guess I am sometimes.' His temper spent, the tension faded from the room.

'Here, let me help you with this stuff,' Jesse said, picking up a toilet seat at his feet. It was the ugliest shade of purple Jesse had ever seen. He held it up and looked quizzically at Phil.

Phil shrugged. 'Hey, if people will buy it, I'll sell it.'

Jesse laughed appreciatively. As the two men started to clean up the clutter, Jesse turned serious. 'You know, Phil, the Police Department doesn't want to admit it, but they're really impressed by what you've done in this neighbourhood. You got the whole place organized a lot better than the police could have done.'

'That's for sure,' Phil replied.

'That's why I think we should work together.'

Phil snickered. 'What, on your Neighbourhood Watch Programme? Listen, Mach, maybe you mean well, but it just wouldn't work around here. Look at those people out there,' he said, pointing out the window. Jesse looked out at all the men, women, and children outside, watching the argument with eager expressions, as if waiting for blood to flow. 'Those people have pride in their neighbourhood again. They're fighting back, they care. And you know why? Because they know they have to take care of themselves now. They can't count on the cops or anybody else to do stuff for them. I'm not going to take that away from them.'

'Phil, we're not asking you to dismantle your organization. And we don't want to take it over, either. We want to work with you. What you've done here has effectively given us an extra fleet of squad cars to patrol this neighbourhood. With your people watching the streets, that frees up the police to handle the real emergencies.'

'That might make sense elsewhere,' Phil admitted, 'but I don't know that we really need the cops around here at all. We seem to have the neighbourhood under control pretty well ourselves.'

'Look, Phil, I'd like to get you some police radios. That way, if you want the cops, we're there for you. And I'll arrange it so the police don't hassle you any more.'

'Yeah?' Phil asked suspiciously. 'And what do you want in exchange?'

'No more press conferences.'

Phil considered the matter for a long moment. 'How many radios?' he asked.

Phil finally agreed not to talk to the press any more and 'not to do anything stupid.' The two men shook hands and Jesse left, but the hostile crowd outside seemed to be less forgiving than Phil had been, and they sullenly moved aside as Jesse tried to get back to his car. He wasn't surprised to find himself so unpopular; after all, these people had just seen him fighting with their local hero. But he wasn't quite prepared to have an elderly woman spit on him as he stepped off the curb.

The woman sank back into the crowd and a voice behind Jesse said, 'And the sad thing is, she's not the only one who wants to do that.'

He turned and saw Mary standing on the sidewalk, a caustic smile on her face. Jesse shrugged. 'I guess I better not run for office around here.'

He started across the street and Mary followed him. 'I saw you fighting with my father.'

'I'm sorry about that,' Jesse said as he reached his car. 'But you know, we weren't really fighting. He just had to get some of his frustration out. I hope it didn't upset you.'

'I'm Phil Simpkins' daughter,' Mary said. 'I don't upset easily. He missed, huh?'

Jesse smiled. 'I'm quick.'

'You're lucky,' Mary countered. 'Are you going to help my father?'

'I'm trying. But I'm not so sure he wants my help.'

'Help him anyway,' Mary said. Jesse looked at her curiously. 'Don't get me wrong. I love my father and I'm really proud of him and what he's done. But he's a stubborn man and once he's made up his mind about something, it's almost impossible to get him to change it. And this

Association is something he's very determined about.'

'He certainly is,' Jesse agreed.

'He's too old to fight another war. And my Mom and I, we don't want to see him get hurt. We don't like to admit it, but every time the phone rings at night, we're afraid it's the police or the hospital calling to tell us something's happened to him. If anyone can help him, you can. My father likes you.'

'What makes you say that?' Jesse asked.

Mary looked at him, a big grin on her face. 'He's never missed before.'

TWENTY-TWO

At first glance, it might appear that there was nothing out of the ordinary at InterCity Warehouse and Depository. Huge eighteen-wheelers were parked outside the main warehouses and men and women in grey uniforms were wheeling material for shipment from the massive buildings into the rear of the waiting trucks. A foreman watched over their work, checking the manifolds on his clipboard as he glanced into each vehicle to make sure every truck was receiving the correct freight. On the shipping dock lay a ghetto blaster, large as a briefcase, an old Little Richard tune blaring out of its tinny speaker. No one seemed unduly concerned this afternoon.

It was only if one looked at the smaller building a couple of hundred yards to the north that one would suspect something was amiss. The building was locked and secure, and two armed guards stood outside the door. They looked straight ahead, like soldiers at attention, intent on their duties.

There were two more guards standing at the front gate. Their attention was on the street and the cars cruising past the area. They too seemed serious and intent; nothing would get past them.

The two guards were not aware that, even as they watched the street, they too were being watched. A black van was parked a block away and Dumos, sitting in the front seat, was surveying the premises through a pair of high-powered binoculars. Albert, at the wheel, said, 'See? I told you they put on a couple of extra guards.'

'No matter,' Dumos said coldly. 'We can still handle them.'

'Maybe we should hit someplace else,' Albert suggested. 'Or maybe we just shouldn't make a hit at all tonight.'

'No!' Dumos barked. 'We will go ahead with the operation as planned. I intend to make a few refinements to take care of the extra guards, but otherwise everything will proceed as scheduled.'

'What about Street Hawk? If he shows up again, that could wreck everything.'

Dumos turned his steel blue gaze at Albert and said nothing, making his lieutenant feel incredibly small and stupid. Dumos didn't like to be reminded about Street Hawk.

'If Street Hawk shows up again, he will have to be taken care of,' Dumos said quietly as he raised the binoculars again. 'I have a surprise in store for him. Now let's get back to the garage.'

Albert started up the vehicle and headed back to headquarters. He wasn't about to question Dumos further, not when he was in one of these moods. He had too much sense for that.

Although Dumos hid it under his cold and methodical features, this was the angriest Albert had ever seen him. It was the angriest Dumos had been in years. Street Hawk had disrupted his schedule last night and forced him to leave millions of dollars' worth of gold behind. Nobody ever disrupted Dumos' schedules and lived to brag about it. He actually hoped that Street Hawk would be foolish enough to come after them again tonight, so he could exact his revenge.

One of Dumos' rules of thumb was that to defeat an enemy, it was important to learn as much about him as one could, so the first thing he'd done that morning was to go to the public library and do some research on his prospective opponent. He gleaned what he could from the various newspapers and magazine articles, and although much of the information was imprecise and full of hyperbole, a few facts did emerge. Despite the accusations the police had levelled against Street Hawk and his so-called 'vigilante' activities, he seemed to be a great believer in the legal system. He turned his various quarries over to the police, often leaving them suspects who, although they first seemed guiltless, were later proved to be tied in with crimes the police had under investigation. The motorcycle was equipped with a number of powerful weapons, but as far as Dumos could tell, he had never killed anybody.

Dumos was particularly struck by the account of Bingham's capture he read in the papers. Bingham had been armed and was extremely dangerous, and when Street Hawk got the drop on him, he could easily have killed him and pleaded self-defence. Instead, he had been content with scaring him into surrendering. Dumos had no intention of making the same mistake. He doubted it would come down to a face-to-face confrontation, but if it did, his knowledge that Street Hawk was not a killer would give him an enormous advantage. No matter how he was threatened, all Dumos had to do was keep his cool and he would come out on top. Calmness and method would win every time.

A honk of the horn snapped Dumos out of his reverie. A car making a left turn from the wrong lane had cut them off momentarily, and Albert waved his fist out the window as the errant driver zipped around the corner. Dumos frowned. Albert was a little bit too nervous, too uncertain, for his taste. Still, he had served him well. Albert was a very reliable lieutenant. He had been the one to locate the rest of the group Dumos used in his operations. Rather than keeping one group with him all the time, he preferred to hire local hoods in whatever city he was operating in at the time. That way, he didn't have to worry about some uppity henchman deciding he could operate just as efficiently without Dumos and trying to take over the gang. Nor did he have to split the gold with anyone else; the kind of men he dealt with usually preferred to take their earnings in a lump sum of cash rather than take the risk of trying to get a fair price for the gold bars without attracting the attention of the authorities.

Dumos didn't like splitting the gold with others. To him,

it represented more than mere wealth. It was power. He had his own overseas sources for turning the gold into cash, but the great majority of his booty was stored on a small Caribbean island he intended to purchase. Once he'd accumulated enough capital, he planned to set up his own government and military, and after that, there was no telling what heights he might rise to. Dumos had dreams, big dreams, dreams of wealth and power and conquest. He had always believed he was a member of that small élite which changed the world to fit their own visions. And after a few more robberies, he intended to make some of those changes a reality.

But just as all journeys begin with a single step, Dumos knew that before he could bring his grandoise plans to fruition, he had to worry about the more mundane matters of pulling off tonight's theft. And that meant taking care of Street Hawk or anyone else who might dare disrupt his plans.

Albert pulled the van into the garage that served as Dumos' headquarters. It had once been an auto body shop, but Dumos had purchased it last month so he could have a central spot as a base of operations. The building was now filled with blueprints and charts and three-dimensional mockups of the places Dumos intended to hit, as well as his cache of weapons. It was here that he had trained his men, drilling into them the minutest details of what he intended to do each evening and how they would cope with anything unexpected that might occur. He taught them to behave like soldiers, trusting his orders implicitly and obeying them without the slightest hesitation.

His henchmen were sitting around a table, playing cards, when Dumos and Albert arrived. As Dumos climbed out of the van, one of the men said, 'You got a visitor,' and pointed to a man sitting on a wooden crate against the wall. His uniform identified him as a corporal in the United States Army.

'You're early,' Dumos said. 'You weren't supposed to be here until three o'clock.'

The corporal shrugged. 'Hey, I gotta be back at the base sooner than I expected. Your time's not always your own in the army, you know. You got the money?'

'Of course,' Dumos said. The other men in the room watched this verbal exchange with interest. He had not yet told them about the extra piece of hardware he would be bringing along on the expedition tonight. 'And you?'

'It's outside, in the truck,' the corporal explained.

Dumos nodded and he and the corporal went out in the street.

A small military truck was parked behind the building. The corporal pulled aside the green canvas that covered the back of the vehicle and Dumos climbed inside. At his feet lay the piece of equipment he had paid this greedy soldier to steal for him: an M20A1 anti-tank free flight missile launcher, also known by the military as the 'Super Bazooka'. It fired a high explosive rocket capable of penetrating up to three hundred millimetres of steel.

The corporal stood outside the truck, watching him. 'Okay, I came through,' he said. 'Now, where's the money?'

'It's inside,' Dumos replied. 'We'll get it in a moment.'

He crouched down and studied his latest acquisition. A cruel smile crept across his face as he lovingly ran his fingers along the barrel of the powerful weapon. Now everything could proceed as he'd intended. Street Hawk was as good as dead.

TWENTY-THREE

'Look at that bozo,' said the long-haired college student standing on the corner. His girlfriend shook her head and laughed. There were about a dozen people in all standing there and with great amusement they were watching a tall man with rust-coloured hair shouting into an open manhole in the centre of the street. There were red flags and pylons all around him, placed there to warn traffic and pedestrians of the danger presented by the open hole, but actually serving to call additional attention to the man in the street.

A middle-aged woman with a shopping bag said, 'That's so sad. Somebody should do something for that poor man.' Several people around her echoed that sentiment, even as they continued to titter.

Jesse was on his way to the Command Centre when he noticed the crowd on the corner. He slowed down as he spotted the object of their ridicule, and for a moment, he considered taking the fellow downtown to have a talk with the police psychiatrist. Then his jaw dropped open and his eyes almost jumped out of their sockets as he recognized the man.

It was Norman.

'Somebody answer me!' Norman was shouting insistently. 'You can't just stay down there and ignore me. I'm a customer of the phone company, I pay my bills every month, and I deserve some answers.'

A voice came back, loud enough for Norman, and no one else, to hear. It shouted an epithet rarely printed in family newspapers or heard in U-rated motion pictures. Norman turned red.

'I heard that!' he shrieked. 'You can't talk to me that way!' Norman pulled a pad and pencil out of his jacket. 'I want your name, mister! I want it now!'

Jesse rolled down his window and shouted to Norman. 'Norman! Come on, get in the car!'

'I'm not leaving here until I get some answers,' Norman insisted.

'Norman, you're talking to a sewer,' Jesse pointed out.

Norman looked up. He suddenly realized he had gathered quite a crowd and they were all laughing at him. He blushed and straightened his tie, trying to recover his composure. He walked toward Jesse's car, chin up, hoping he appeared like the calm professional he imagined himself to be.

As he reached Jesse's car, a little boy walked up to him and said, 'Don't let them bother you, mister. I talk to holes all the time.'

Stripped of his last shred of dignity, Norman quickly climbed in the car and slammed the door behind him. He sank down in his seat. 'I don't know what's the matter with me,' he said.

Jesse drove off. 'You're just tired and frustrated. It happens to all of us.'

'Not to me. I'm usually quite stable.' Norman suddenly realized the car was moving. 'Where are we going?' he asked.

'Well, I know this great manhole over on Sixteenth Street. I figured we'd get a sixpack and drive over there. You can yell at it while I work out how to get a list of gold depositories.'

Norman gave him a dirty look. 'I don't think that's very funny.'

Jesse shook his head. 'Hey come on, Norman, you're taking this much too seriously.'

'I am, am I? Did I make jokes when you couldn't come up with a date last weekend? Let's see now, how many girls did you call?'

162

'Hey, don't even kid me about something like that.'

'You see? You see how sensitive you are when I start making jokes about your girlfriends?'

'I don't really think you can compare computers and women.'

'It's all relative. You and I just have different priorities.' Norman looked out the window, pretending to ignore his companion.

Jesse sighed. 'Okay, Norman, you're right. I'm sorry. I know your computers are as important to you as my girlfriends are to me. I think it's a little weird, but hey, different strokes, right? Seriously, though, when do you think your computers will be working again?'

Norman shrugged his shoulders. 'I have no idea. The only human being I've been able to talk to is that fellow working underground back there, and all he did was call me a foul name. You wouldn't believe what he called me, Jesse.'

'I probably would,' Jesse replied, smiling. He doubted he had called him anything Jesse hadn't wanted to call Norman at one time or another. 'But I have a problem. Altobelli has declared all information concerning gold shipments off-limits to anyone but necessary personnel. And I didn't want to risk calling any extra attention to myself by trying to get the information some other way. So I was kind of hoping the computers would be operational by now so we could get what we needed from them.'

'Well, if the phone company ever finished, it would only take a minute to get a list of gold depositories. But until they do, I'm pretty helpless.'

Jesse slowed down as they neared the Command Centre. 'Norman, if the computers were operational, who would you tap into?'

'I don't know. The Federal Reserve or the Treasury.'

'What's their address?'

Eyes widening, Norman turned to him. 'Why?'

'If we can't tap into their computers, we'll just have to go there in person. You've got friends on the inside.'

'I've got friends in the Defence Department!' Norman shouted. 'Not the Treasury!'

'Big deal. It's all the same government, isn't it?'

'Jesse, Street Hawk is an undercover operation. That means we stay undercover!' He slapped his hand with his fist to emphasize the point.

'Norman,' Jesse explained patiently, as if to a child, 'we're a team, right? My job is to ride Street Hawk and your job is to acquire the information necessary for us to operate effectively. Now I've come to trust and rely on your ability to do practically anything. You wouldn't want to break that trust, now would you?'

'Jesse—'

'And it seems only fair to me that since it's your half of the operation that's messed up, you should come up with some other way of getting the information. Now I've suggested one method. If you have a better suggestion, I'll be happy to hear it.'

Norman sat back in his seat and sighed. 'Make a right at the corner.'

Jesse cracked a smile. 'Where are we going?'

Norman looked utterly worn and defeated. 'The Federal Building.'

The Federal Building was an imposing structure of steel and concrete that rose twenty stories into the air. The building contained nothing but government offices and it operated almost exclusively from the hours of eight in the morning to half past five in the afternoon. A veritable army of employees worked inside and they seemed to spend most of their time either trying to get information or action out of one of the other offices or preventing some federal bureaucrat from getting information or action out of their own. Entire forests had been wiped out to make the paper upon which the government workers typed their barely comprehensible reports, which were then sent on to a higher office where they would be duly filed, unread, and never again see the light of day. The worst part of the whole thing, though, was the knowledge that things were much worse in Washington.

Jesse had to drive through the heavy downtown traffic to reach his destination and it was late afternoon by the time he finally pulled into the underground parking garage that served the building's employees. As Jesse parked, Norman said, 'I think you better wait in the car.'

'What? Why?'

'I'd just feel better handling this myself,' Norman explained.

'But what if you need help?' asked Jesse.

'Look, you wanted me to get the information for you, right? So I'm getting it. But you have to let me do it my way.'

Jesse sighed. 'All right. I'll wait in the car.' He flipped on his tape player and Norman hurried out of the car before he had to be subjected to any more of Jesse's dreadful rock and roll music. He wasn't very happy about this whole business, but the last thing he felt he needed when dealing with the Federal Government was to have Jesse Mach standing behind him the whole time, making suggestions on how he would bypass the entire system.

The enormous lobby was deserted save for an attentive-looking man sitting at a desk by the wall further from the door. A sign on his desk promised Information so Norman crossed the wide expanse and asked the man where he could find the Treasury Department.

The man pointed back toward the door. 'There's a directory over that that will tell you where all the offices are.'

Norman was confused. 'Then what are you here for?'

The man straightened up proudly, as if his was a job vital to the nation's security. 'I tell people where the directory is,' he explained.

'It figures,' Norman mumbled as he walked back to the directory. He located the Treasury Department and took the elevator to the twelfth floor. As he walked down the hallway, he could hear the sounds of hundreds of typewriters clicking away from behind closed doors. The walls were adorned with portraits of men in business suits, like a bureaucrats' Hall of Fame, and Norman couldn't help but wonder how people could stand to work here. He wished his computers were working again; Norman hated the real world.

He found the Treasury Department and stepped in. There was a small waiting room with an uncomfortable

wooden bench against the wall, and a grey-haired bespec-
tacled woman pounding the typewriter behind the counter.
Norman waited patiently for the woman to look up.

She didn't. She kept typing away as if he wasn't there at
all. Finally, Norman interrupted her work. 'Excuse me,
could you help me a minute?'

The woman ceased her typing and looked up at him, a
crooked frown on her face. 'You have to take a number, sir,'
she said. Her voice sounded like nails on a chalkboard,
thought not as pleasant.

There was a sign on the wall that read, 'Please Take a
Number for Service'. It looked more like the kind of sign
one would find in an ice cream parlour than an office of the
Federal Government.

'I'm the only one here,' Norman pointed out.

'I'm sorry, sir, you still have to take a number. Those are
the rules.'

Norman sighed and took a number. The woman went
back to her typing, ignoring Norman again. He sat down on
the wooden bench. He had a feeling he was going to have a
long wait.

TWENTY-FOUR

Jesse was still out in his car an hour later, waiting for Norman to return. He drummed his fingers impatiently on the dashboard and looked at his watch. This was a waste of time. He still had to finish up with this Simpkins business this afternoon so he could be free to tackle his weightier problems that night. He couldn't afford to lose the rest of the day sitting in a parking lot.

'Well Norman, you're a big boy now,' he said aloud. 'I guess you'll have to get home by yourself.' He started up the car and headed back to the police station.

After checking to make sure he hadn't received any phone calls while he was out, Jesse went down to the Requisitions Office in the basement. Requisitions was run by a constantly dieting brunette named Denise. She had been one of Jesse's closest friends when he was a motorcycle cop and he could recall countless occasions when he had wooed out of her some piece of equipment that was reserved for someone else. That's what he figured he had to do now. Altobelli wasn't going to be too happy with the idea of giving Simpkins all those radios he'd promised him.

Denise was chewing a piece of sugarless gum when Jesse walked in the door. Her eyes lit up at the sight of him and she bounced out of her seat and ran over to give him a hug. 'Jesse! You came down to visit me! I never see you any more.'

167

The room where Denise held court contained one desk and forty-eight almost perennially empty shelves. In principle, the shelves were supposed to be fully stocked at all times, but in practice, material was in such short supply that things were usually snapped up within a day after they arrived.

'Hey, these days the only things I need are typewriter ribbons and paper,' Jesse explained. 'There's not much call for me to come down here.'

'You could come down to visit,' Denise said, sticking out her lower lip.

'I'm sorry, you're right. I should come down more often. But listen, Denise, this is really a business call. You know those six new police radios you received the other day? I need them.'

Denise shook her head. 'I'm sorry, Jesse, but those radios are supposed to go to Special Services.'

'No, no, there's been a change. They're supposed to go to me now. Altobelli said so.'

'Oh, well in that case, it's all right.' She pulled open a drawer and handed Jesse a requisition form. 'Fill this out, have Altobelli sign it, and the radios are yours.'

Jesse looked at the form. 'Altobelli has to sign it?'

Denise nodded. 'Of course. I already have a requisition form from Special Services. I need his written authorization to override that.'

Jesse frowned. 'Do we really have to bother with all this red tape? We're friends, Denise.'

'Sorry. Rules are rules.'

Jesse walked behind Denise and started massaging the back of her neck. 'Hey Denise, remember that time I took you to that Italian restaurant up in the hills? You know, the place with the view?'

'Mmm-hmm,' she said, remembering.

'And afterwards we took that drive along the beach and I parked the car and we went swimming.'

Denise nodded. 'A little lower,' she pleaded. Jesse moved his hands down her back and she drew in her breath. 'Oh, that's it,' she moaned.

He leaned over and whispered in her ear. 'And then we

went back to your place and I built the fire and we sat and watched the logs burn.'

'I remember,' she giggled.

'Now, how about those radios?'

'Fill out the form, have Altobelli sign it, and the radios are yours.'

Jesse stopped his massage. 'Thanks a lot, Denise,' he said sarcastically.

'Hey, things are tough all over.'

Jesse showed up in Altobelli's office a few minutes later.

'Excuse me, Commander, I need your signature on this.' He put the completed form on Altobelli's desk.

Altobelli picked up his pen and looked over the form. He read about half of it before he looked up at Jesse and asked gruffly, 'What the hell is this, Mach? What do you need six radios for?'

'They're for Simpkins, sir.'

'Simpkins?' Altobelli was utterly appalled. 'Why told you to give him radios?'

'You did, sir.' Altobelli raised his eyebrows. 'You told me to offer him anything I liked as long as it got him to shut up. So I did.'

Altobelli looked disgusted but he returned to the form. He read a little further and then shouted out, 'Wait a second!' He shot up in his chair. 'This is for those six new radios we just got in! What did you promise him new ones for? Do you have any idea what they cost?'

'Yes I do, they're—'

'They're over eight hundred dollars apiece. And six of them, that's—'

'—four thousand, nine hundred sixty-one dollars and eighty-four cents, sir,' Jesse said, finishing his sentence. 'Including tax.'

'Yeah. That much. Forget it, Mach. We're not spending that kind of dough on Simpkins.'

'Sir, those are the only radios available,' Jesse started.

Altobelli interrupted him. 'And I already promised them to Lieutenant James over in Special Services. What do I tell him, huh? If he doesn't get those radios, he'll have a fit.'

'The way I look at it, Commander, you have a very simple choice to make. Which one of them can yell louder?'

'Simpkins,' Altobelli admitted.

'And which one of them gets more press coverage?'

'Simpkins,' Altobelli admitted again.

'And which one of them is worse for your ulcers?'

'Simpkins,' Altobelli admitted still again.

'So,' Jesse said, summing up his case, 'which one of them gets the radios?'

Altobelli opened his drawer and took out a roll of antacid tablets. He popped one into his mouth. 'Does it have to be those radios?' he pleaded. 'Can't we give him radios later on? Lieutenant James has been bugging me about them for months.'

'Sure, we can wait,' Jesse conceded. 'But in the meantime, I can't guarantee that Simpkins won't decide to have another press conference. Or two, or three. . .'

'Okay, okay, I get the picture,' Altobelli grumbled. He picked up the pen and prepared to sign the form. He looked up at Jesse once more. 'So if we give these radios to Simpkins, he'll start cooperating with us?'

'Well, not exactly. All he's promised to do is to stop giving press conferences. Oh, and I told him the police wouldn't hassle his organization any more, either.'

'You would,' Altobelli commented in a tone of disgust. 'So how much is cooperation going to cost? A couple of squad cars?'

'You're making it sound like extortion.'

'It is. How much?'

'Well, all he's really said is that he'll think it over. But I look at these radios as kind of a gesture of good faith. You know, showing him we're both on the same side. And the way I figure it, if he's got the radios with him, it will make it more likely that he'll call us instead of trying to take care of things on his own.'

Jesse's beeper went off just then. That meant Norman must have finally returned from the Federal Building. Jesse smiled apologetically. 'My service wants me to call in.'

'Another hot date, Mach?' Altobelli asked caustically. He

reluctantly scrawled his signature on the bottom of the form. 'You know, this really isn't fair. You end up with a quiet plumber and I get an angry lieutenant.'

'Next time we'll switch, sir,' Jesse said. He took the form and went back to his own office.

Once there, he put a call in to the Command Centre. He could tell by the way Norman answered the phone that he wasn't in the best of moods. 'Hi, Norman. You're mad, aren't you?'

'I had to take the bus back!' Norman shouted.

'I'm sorry about that—'

'The bus, Jesse! Do you have any idea what it's like to take the bus at rush hour?'

'No, I don't,' Jesse admitted. 'I have a car.'

'Well, it's not an experience I'd like to repeat in the near future.'

'Did you get the information, Norman?'

'Yeah, I got it—'

'Good. I'll be over there as soon as I can.'

Jesse hung up the phone. Norman was getting rather testy. Jesse supposed that was what happened when a computer wizard went through withdrawal.

He went back to the basement and presented the signed form to Denise. She studied Altobelli's signature warily.

'Are you sure you didn't forge this?' she asked.

'Are you kidding? If I had, it would be legible.'

The gum cracked in Denise's mouth. She pulled the six radios off an otherwise empty shelf and handed them to Jesse. 'Be careful with them,' she cautioned. 'I don't know when we'll be able to get more.'

'Thanks,' Jesse said. He tucked the radios under his arm and headed out the door. He'd drop them off at Phil's and then he'd be free to concentrate all his attention on those gold robbers.

He had no intention of letting them get away from him again.

TWENTY-FIVE

Street lights blinked on all over the city as the sky gradually darkened. The night seemed preternaturally quiet, the stillness only occasionally shattered by the honking of a car horn or the barking of a dog. It was as if the entire city was bracing itself for some explosive act of violence that would light up the sky.

There were several cars parked along the street in front of Phil Simpkins' shop. They all bore the bald eagle logo on their doors, signifying their owners were members of Simpkins' organization. Every few minutes, another car would arrive, and a blue-jacketed man would walk into Phil's shop. The street was dark; all the other shops were closed and the only light on the entire block came through Phil's window. As his place began to fill with men, Phil closed the curtain, shutting out even this last vestige of light. He turned to the other men.

'We're waiting for Abe and Joey,' he explained. 'As soon as they get here, we can get started.'

A few of the men were eating submarine sandwiches and drinking coffee. Phil's desk was covered with empty cups and breadcrumbs and he walked over to brush them off.

The door opened and Abe and Joey walked in. 'Sorry we're late,' Joey said.

'So am I,' Abe seconded. 'My wife made lasagna for dinner tonight.'

Several men in the room groaned. Mrs Weinstein's lasagna was infamous.

Phil looked around the room. 'Okay, we're all here now,' she said. 'Joey, you got the list?'

'Yeah.' Joey handed him a sheet of paper on which were printed the names of all the places where gold was being stored at the present time. 'There're eight of them,' he explained. 'That's too many to try to look out for.'

'Yeah, eight is an awful lot,' Phil agreed. 'Are you sure about these?'

'Yeah, I'm sure,' Joey insisted, pulling a candy bar out of his pocket. 'I got the truck info from Gleason over at the Union. Johnny Zecca from the Transportation Commission gave my brother the info on the warehouse, and the rest of the stuff comes from Richie's wife. She works at the main office at the Federal Bank.'

Phil nodded, feeling fairly pleased with himself. He looked at Abe. 'You see? What did I tell you? We got a network of information as effective as the cops any day.' He studied the list. 'Well, there's no point in trying to watch all these places. We should only worry about those that are actually in the neighbourhood. That's these three.' He put checkmarks next to three of the names on the list, including InterCity.

'Phil, would you stop being so mysterious and start telling us what's going on?' asked Frankie Cusimano, the man who'd asked Phil about the jackets earlier that afternoon.

'We're going to go after those gold robbers,' Phil replied. 'If they try another hit in this neighbourhood, they're going to run into some heavy opposition.'

Frankie looked scared. 'Hey, I didn't know we were going to start messing in anything like that.'

'Relax,' Phil assured him. 'You new men, I want you to just go out on regular patrols, like we do every night. But those of us who are old hands at this—' he nodded at Abe and Joey and a couple of the other men '—I want us to concentrate on the area near these warehouses. We'll patrol the streets, looking for any suspicious cars, anything that don't look right. And then we'll—'

There was a knock at the door and Phil stopped speaking. He surveyed the room, double-checking that there was no one missing from the group. Seeing that they were all there, he told Ted, the man nearest the door, to have a peek through the curtains and see who was outside.

Ted pulled the curtain aside and looked out. 'It's that cop that was here this afternoon, Phil.'

'Oh, Mach,' Phil said. 'He must have my radios. Let him in.'

Ted opened the door and Jesse stepped in.

A dozen pairs of eyes turned silently in his direction and Jesse could feel the waves of distrust and suspicion radiating toward him. He grinned, trying to alleviate some of the tension. 'Hey, am I still persona non grata around here?'

No one spoke for a second, and then Phil stepped forward. 'Hey, come on guys, that's no way to treat Jesse. He's on our side now.'

With Phil's permission, the other men in the room were now able to relax a little bit. Jesse stepped forward and set the six brand-new radios down on his desk.

'Here're the radios, Phil. Just like I promised.'

'Radios?' Joey asked. This was the first time he, or any of the other men in the room besides Phil, had heard about the radios.

'Police radios,' Jesse explained. 'Phil's always complaining about how difficult it is to get in touch with the police by phone. Well, now you don't need phones. You guys run into trouble, you just contact the police dispatcher and he'll send you help. You'll have the same priority as any police officer would.'

Several of the men in the room started to smile. They felt good about this visible display of respect from the Police Department.

'Well, thanks a lot, Jesse,' Phil said. 'These radios will come in real handy. I'd offer you a cup of coffee or something, but as you can see, we're having a little meeting here, so I'll talk to you later, all right?'

Jesse's eyes dropped down to Phil's desk and he caught a glimpse of the list of gold depositories. He only had time to make out the first name on the list before Phil flipped it over.

'Yeah, right,' Jesse said. He nodded to Phil and a few of the other men, and left the shop. The door closed behind him and he heard someone turning the key.

As Jesse reached his car, he turned around and looked at the darkened plumbing shop. They were up to something in there, something they didn't want the police to know about. And from the single name he'd read off Joey's list, Jesse could make a pretty fair guess as to what it might be. Part of him felt constrained to go back in and issue yet another warning to Phil, but another part of him thought that perhaps Street Hawk could make use of Simpkins' organization. And with Norman's computers still out of whack, Street Hawk could use all the help he could get.

Inside the shop, the tension in the room had completely dissipated with Jesse's departure. Abe picked up one of the radios and looked at it, smiling. 'That's a relief,' he said. 'For a minute there, I thought you actually expected us to take care of those gold robbers ourselves.'

'I do,' Phil said.

Abe looked up, surprised. 'But the radios—'

'Oh, sure,' Phil interrupted, 'if things really get out of hand, I guess we can call the cops. But as far as I'm concerned, they're the last resort, not the first. The cops have already had plenty of chances to get these guys and they've blown it every time. Now it's our turn. And we're gonna catch them.'

'What with?' Abe asked. 'Plungers?'

'Abe's right,' Ted said. 'I don't know about the rest of you, but I ain't had a legitimate fight since my brother-in-law moved out nine years ago. I ain't ready to take on some big-time mobsters.'

'They're not big-time,' Phil insisted. 'They're small-time punks, no different from any of the other punks we've taken on. We can handle them.'

Abe shook his head. 'I don't know, Phil. These guys are supposed to be awful dangerous. They'll have guns.'

Phil walked over to a wooden cabinet against the wall. He slid open the door, revealing a row of shotguns lined up like battle-ready soldiers. 'So will we,' he announced.

The room was quiet as the men gazed in awe at the un-expected cache of firearms. Phil said, 'I'm not asking anybody who doesn't know how to use one or who doesn't like them to take a gun. But I'm taking one. If those gold robbers show up around here, I mean to be prepared. The way I look at it, we can't afford to let any hoods at all come around here. If we go after the street gangs and leave these other guys alone, that'll be like saying this neighbourhood is safe for hoods as long as they bring enough weapons with them. That's not right. If we really want to keep this area safe, we gotta prove we're not afraid of anybody.'

Phil pulled out one of the shotguns and placed it over his shoulder. He looked at the others, waiting for another to make a move.

Joey said, 'Well, I used to do a lot of hunting. I guess it wouldn't hurt to have one along.'

He stepped forward and took out a shotgun. The others began to move toward the cabinet and Phil handed out the guns to all their eager, grasping hands.

Abe was the only one who didn't want a gun, and even he ultimately agreed to take one after the other men talked him into it. 'I don't know, all this business with guns, it might be more dangerous to have them than not to have them,' he said. He walked over to the cabinet and took the last of the weapons. 'But I don't think those guys will show up anyway, and if it'll make the rest of you happy, I'll take one.'

'If you run into them,' Phil promised, 'you'll be glad you have it along. Believe me.' The men stood with guns at their shoulders, and as Phil looked them over, he felt like he was back in the army again. 'Okay, men, now I want everybody to keep Channel Six open. If you see anything suspicious, you shout out and the rest of us will come running.'

There were nods of agreement all around the room. Phil walked over to the map and marked the location of the three warehouses on it. 'Okay,' he said, 'now for our assignments. . .'

TWENTY-SIX

Jesse could tell Norman was still angry. When he finally showed up at the Command Centre, Norman was sitting at the darkened console with his back to him, not even acknowledging his presence. Jesse waited for Norman to say something, but when he refused to even turn around, Jesse approached him and slapped him lightly on the back.

'Hey, come on, Norman, you're not still mad at me, are you?'

Norman whirled around, glaring at Jesse like a petulant child. 'You were supposed to wait for me!' he pouted.

'I waited over an hour,' Jesse explained. 'You didn't come out.'

'These things take time. I couldn't just go in there and demand information. I had to work through the proper channels.' Jesse bit his lip, but he knew he had to let Norman get this out of his system or he'd never hear the end of it. 'I had to see four different people in that office before I found somebody who even had the right information, and even then I ended up having to call Kirby in Defence and he had to call his boss, and his boss had to call the Treasury Department in Washington and then Washington called the local office . . . and then they released the information to me. Obviously, that's going to take longer than an hour.'

Jesse shook his head. 'I hate red tape.'

'Well, you're an employee of the Federal Government now, and that means you have to get used to working within the system.'

'Okay, okay,' Jesse conceded. He didn't feel like arguing anymore. 'The bottom line is you got the information we needed, right?'

Norman spread a computer printout across the control console. 'All I got were the locations of the Federal gold depositories. We still need more background on the robberies. Then I can analyze the statistics, come up with some probabilities, and hopefully determine which depository will be hit.'

'Sounds good,' Jesse said. 'Let's do it.'

'I can't. I need the computer.'

Jesse sighed. 'Well, then let's not worry about determining probabilities right now. Let's try to figure out a way how I can cover the gold depositories.' He studied the computer printout. 'How many are there?'

'There's eight of them, Jesse. That's too many for you to cover all by yourself. Without the computer, we don't have a chance.'

Jesse said, 'Norman, this hunk of metal and plastic cannot replace a human being. It's just a mechanism, built by people to help people. We can break it, we can fix it, we can turn it off, or we can turn it on.'

'Not on,' Norman pointed out. 'Not right now, anyway.'

'Look, I'm not saying it wouldn't be easier if we had the computer, I'm just saying we can still get the job done without it.'

Norman looked at Jesse, then looked down at the printout, reading the locations of the various depositories around the city. 'These places are all over town,' he pointed out. 'You're going to have to spend the whole night riding from one to the other.'

'So what? I did it last night, didn't I?'

'Last night, we only had four to worry about. And even then, the thieves got away.' He shook his head. 'Without the computers—'

'Norman, I'm going out!' Jesse insisted. 'Now if you

want to help me, that's fine. Otherwise, I'll go it alone!'

'Of course I'm going to help you. I'm not letting you take Street Hawk out without some backup, even if the machines are down. What do you want me to do?'

'Well, while I'm out on the streets, you should monitor the police band and see if you hear anything. And also monitor CB Channel Six.'

Norman wrinkled his brow. 'Why?'

'That's the channel Phil Simpkins and his group are using. I got a funny feeling those guys might just spot the gold robbers before the cops do.'

'A funny feeling? That's hardly scientific.'

'Sometimes you just have to go with your gut instincts, Norman,' Jesse replied. He turned his attention back to the list of depositories. 'Now what we've got to do is map out a route between these warehouses so I can cut my travel time down to a minimum.'

'I'll take care of that. In the meantime, you go suit up.'

Jesse smiled. 'Thanks, Norman.'

A squad car was slowly cruising down the quiet, residential street. Inside, two police officers surveyed the area, looking for signs of trouble but doubting they'd find any. Under the dashboard, a police radio crackled out a constant stream of information, and the cops kept one ear cocked toward it in case an emergency call came in from someplace in the area.

They heard a banging up ahead and the policeman on the passenger side trained a flashlight out the window toward the sound of the disturbance. Captured in the halo of light was a German Shepherd dog, nosing around in a garbage can he'd just knocked over. The officer shut off the flashlight. 'Somebody should keep that thing on a leash,' he said.

The other policeman spotted Phil Simpkins' car at the intersection in front of them, the Protection Association eagle on the door clearly visible in their headlights. He nudged his partner and pointed at the car. 'Better call it in,' he suggested.

The first policeman picked up the mike and radioed in to the dispatcher. 'Dispatch, this is Charlie Four. We got the

Twelfth Street Protection Association cruising the streets. You want us to run them home?'

'Negative,' came the reply over the wire. 'They have authorization.'

The officer shrugged and hung the mike back up by the radio. 'Somebody should put those guys on a leash, too.'

The two officers might have been more reluctant to let the car pass by had they been able to see the two shotguns inside the vehicle, lying on the front seat between Phil and Joey. Joey was looking out the window, chewing on a candy bar and studying the street with the same fervency the police had exhibited. Phil had one hand on the wheel and the other one on the CB mike.

'Ted, how's it look out there?' he said, calling the car that was watching the Western Warehouse.

'All quiet over here,' Ted replied.

'How about you, Abe?' Phil continued. Abe was patrolling the area around Coast Storage. 'You got anything?'

'Heartburn. I ate too much of my wife's lasagna.'

Joey laughed, but Phil just looked angry. 'Come on, Abe, this is serious,' he said.

'So is this! Have you ever tasted my wife's lasagna?'

Phil hung up the mike, disgusted. He said, 'Let's take another circle around InterCity and make sure all's quiet over there.'

Back at the Command Centre, Norman was monitoring Phil as well as the police, just as Jesse had suggested. As soon as Phil went off the air, Norman radioed Jesse. 'What's happening out there?' he asked.

'Everything's quiet,' Jesse responded. He was miles away, on the north side of the city, and thus far he hadn't even run into a mugging or a burglary. It was as if every criminal in town was taking the night off. 'You picking up anything?'

'Nothing,' Norman answered. 'It's quiet everywhere. But I'll keep listening.'

Things would not remain quiet for long. Even as Norman and Jesse were assuring each other the streets were peaceful, Albert's black van was slowly making its way up the road toward InterCity Warehouse. Three masked men sat in the back of the van, their Uzis cradled across their laps, and Albert had his own gun on the seat beside him. About a block away from the front gate, Albert pulled over to the curb and doused his headlights. He spoke into the two-way radio. 'We're in position,' he said.

'Excellent,' came Dumos' response. 'We'll be there shortly.'

Dumos instructed the pilot to head for InterCity. As soon as the chopper took off, he climbed out of his seat and into the back. The M20A1 was mounted on a tripod. Dumos slid open the side door and swung the bazooka around, so it was pointing outside. He was ready now.

The two guards at the front gate of InterCity Warehouse heard the sound of the approaching helicopter and exchanged worried looks; they had been warned to be on the lookout for a 'copter. The two men stepped outside and started to scan the skies.

Suddenly, like some monstrous bird of prey, the helicopter dropped out of the clouds above them. Drawing their revolvers, the men fired them at the menacing apparition over their heads, but their weapons proved to be of little use. The helicopter moved into position, and Dumos aimed the bazooka out the door and fired. The guards saw the bright flash in the door of the 'copter, but before they even had time to wonder what it was, the front gate exploded in a raging storm of fire and smoke. The two guards were knocked to the ground by its force, and wood and other debris showered down on them.

A block away, Albert gunned the engine and shot forward. Bursting through the smoking gate, the van screeched to a halt and an Uzi-armed gunman jumped out, training his weapons on the two guards. Dazed and shaken, the men looked up, saw the gun pointing at them, and raised their hands.

Phil and Joey, on their way to the warehouse, were close enough to hear the sound of the explosion. 'Sounds like something's going on over at InterCity,' Joey said. 'Maybe we should call the cops.'

He picked up the police radio but Phil grabbed his arm.

'No, not yet,' he said as he pressed further down on the accelerator. 'Let's have a look for ourselves, first.'

The explosion had also attracted the notice of the other two guards at InterCity that night. They were in the northernmost building, standing watch over the gold. Although their orders were not to leave their post for anything, the burning, roaring noises outside strained their curiosity and they slipped out the side door to investigate. As they moved toward the front of the building, the black van bowled at them and they were forced to dive out of the way of the thundering vehicle. The two remaining henchmen leapt out of the rear, riddling the ground in front of the guards with machine gun bullets. Faced with superior firepower, the men dropped their lightweight pistols and surrendered.

Phil and Joey had reached the front gate by now. The helicopter was nowhere in sight, but, from the security of their car, they could see the first two guards being marched toward the van by the nylon-masked gunman.

'That's them!' Phil shouted excitedly. 'This is our chance.' He grabbed the CB mike and yelled into it, 'We got those gold guys over at InterCity! Everybody over here on the double!'

Every Association car in the area heard the call. Wherever they were, they stopped, turned around, and headed for the warehouse.

Norman heard the call also. He shouted into his own microphone, 'Jesse! They're at InterCity!' He looked down at the city map spread out in front of him. 'Take Pine Street! It's the fastest way!'

'No, it isn't,' Jesse replied.

The street he was speeding down ran parallel to the city viaduct. During the rainy winter months, the viaduct became a rushing river, but at this time of year, it was little more than a long, concrete thruway with less than an inch of water in it. Jesse hit vertical lift and flew over the fence separating him from the viaduct. He slid down the embankment into the nearly dry riverbed and surged forward. A wall of spray shot out of both sides as he zipped through the shallow water.

'Jesse, what is your location?' Norman shouted.

'Riding the rapids,' Jesse said. 'Unless we get a sudden rainstorm, I'll be there in five minutes.'

Jesse pulled on the throttle, bringing his speed up to its maximum. Norman had said Street Hawk could approach speeds of two hundred miles per hour without computer assist, but Jesse had never had reason to test it before. He was about to find out if it was true.

Back at InterCity, no one as yet had taken notice of Phil and Joey's arrival. The two men watched in horrified fascination as Albert approached each of the guards and they crumpled to the ground. Albert was merely knocking them out with chloroform, but to the men sitting in the car just outside the gate, it looked like he had perfected some silent, mysterious method of killing them. Joey started fiddling with the police radio.

'There's no time for that!' Phil shouted as he plunged through the gate and spun the car around to block the van's escape route. He grabbed one of the shotguns and jumped out of the car, and Joey joined him a second later. Holding their guns at their hips, they faced the thieves, legs spread and bellies sticking over their belts, like some grotesque parody of old Western heroes.

'All right, you punks!' Phil shouted. 'Freeze!'

The gold hijackers slowly turned. There was a moment of tense silence as the two groups of armed men stared at each other over the hundred yards or so that separated them. Phil's finger was on the trigger of his gun, and he was ready to fire if necessary.

Albert surreptitiously brought the radio to his lips. 'We got trouble,' he whispered.

A second later, the helicopter loomed up from behind the warehouse. It hovered there for a second, while Dumos aimed the bazooka, and then fired. Phil and Joey could see the bright flash as the rocket peeled straight toward them, and as they jumped out of the way, it sailed over them and struck Phil's car. With an earthshaking roar, the vehicle went up in a ball of fire and the two men could feel the tongues of flame lick their backs as they scrambled to their feet and ran toward whatever shelter the shadows could provide.

'Kill those clowns!' Dumos barked into the radio.

Albert turned white, but he was too afraid of Dumos to disobey a direct order. 'Find those guys and shoot them!' he cried.

The three henchmen ran into the shadows after them.

Phil and Joey ducked behind a trash dumpster over by the fence. They had heard Albert pronounce their death sentence and they were shaking violently, the blood drained from their faces. 'We should have called the cops,' Phil whispered.

Nodding, Joey pulled out the radio he had prudently tucked under his belt. Phil grabbed it and quickly radioed police headquarters himself. 'Help,' he whispered. 'This is Phil Simpkins. We're at InterCity Warehouse and those gold hijackers are going to kill us!'

The sound of the henchmen's footsteps were getting louder. Phil shut off the radio and shoved it under the dumpster, out of sight. Just as he withdrew his hand, he felt cold steel against his temple and he froze.

'Here they are!' the masked man shouted. 'All right, you two! Get out!'

Raising their hands, Phil and Joey climbed to their feet. They stepped out of their place of concealment and the gunman pushed them out in the light, where Dumos could watch their execution. The other two henchmen joined their companion, and they turned their weapons on their two frightened captives.

'Tell them to shoot!' the impatient Dumos shouted into Albert's radio.

Albert opened his mouth to shout the order, but before he got a word out, he heard a roaring sound from the direction of Phil's burning car, and he turned to look. Like an avenging angel sent from the heavens, Jesse burst through the wall of flame at the front gate, sailing over the fiery automobile with ease. Before he even hit the ground, he started firing his guns, and the three executioners turned away from their prospective victims and returned the gunfire.

Taking advantage of the momentary respite, Phil and

Joey ran back to the relative safety of the trash dumpster.

Bullets whizzing past him, Jesse dodged the gunfire and shot off to the side. The gunsmen started chasing him, but Jesse instantly spun around and surged back toward them, guns blazing at full power. The three gunmen stopped in mid-stride, turned tail, and started running, the fifty calibre slugs kicking up the ground behind them.

Hovering over the scene, Dumos yelled instructions to the pilot and brought his own weapon into range. As soon as he was in position, he fired another missile. Jesse heard the whistling rocket over the sounds of the gunfire and he immediately slammed on the airfoils, braking instantaneously. The shell struck the dirt just in front of him, and the ground rocked with the force of the explosion. The fleeing gunmen fell as the earth seemed to tilt beneath them. They hustled back to their feet and quickly dived for shelter, behind a nearby building.

A column of smoke swirled above the newly-formed crater. Skirting around it, Jesse bore down on the van, where Albert was standing. Dumos' lieutenant grabbed his own Uzi from out of the front seat and started firing at the advancing figure of Street Hawk.

In the air, the chopper circled around and dived at Jesse again. Dumos turned the bazooka, getting the motorcyclist in his sights, and fired. Jesse tore off at an angle, cutting it so close he could actually feel the heat of the shell as it flew past him. With a thundering roar, the missile struck the van, splitting it in two. Caught in the updraft of debris, Albert flew into the air, turned a somersault, and landed on his back, unconscious.

Drifting across the yard was a cloud of smoke, and as Jesse flew into the greyish haze, he effectively camouflaged himself from the view of the helicopter circling in the air above him. Under cover of darkness, the infra-red adapter in his helmet automatically switched on, and Jesse turned his gaze upward, toward the sound of the whirling propellers. He had a clear view of the helicopter and, locking the monocle targeting system on it, he fired the particle beam. The high-powered laser struck one of the skids of the bottom of the chopper, tearing it from its struts. It fell to the earth.

Suddenly out of balance, the pilot lost control of his airborne vehicle. The 'copter spun around as the pilot desperately tried to compensate for the missing skid. Through the front window, Dumos could see the warehouse roof looming toward them and, realizing a crash was imminent, he dived through the open doorway and fell some thirty feet to the ground below. He was unhurt, and he turned his head as he heard the 'copter crash on the nearby roof. It bounced several times before coming to a stop. The pilot stepped out, stumbled for a few steps, and then fell off the roof.

Jesse shot out of the smoky haze and braked to a halt in front of Dumos. Clothed in black, with the smoke swirling around him and the bright flame of the burning van reflected in his helmet, he resembled nothing less than a demon from hell. Dumos looked up at him and then glanced off to the side, where Albert lay unconscious on the ground, his gun just out of reach. Dumos slowly rose to his feet, hands in the air.

Jesse relaxed slightly, and Dumos caught the momentary lapse and dived back to the ground, scooping up the Uzi. Jesse opened up with his gun, bracketing him on either side with machine gun fire. Dumos trembled, clutching the weapon tightly. He was determined to remain in control, despite the tumult and the roar all around him. Bullets whizzed past his ear as he raised the Uzi and aimed it at Jesse's chest.

Jesse could see the determined look in the eye of his opponent. 'Norman, you know that heat test you wanted me to conduct?' he asked.

Miserable over the lost contact and the frightening sounds he was hearing over his headphones, Norman could barely manage a whispered, 'Yes.'

'Well, I'm doing it,' Jesse said, as he fired the particle beam at Dumos' gun. The weapon immediately glowed red-hot, and Dumos screamed, dropping the gun to the ground. He brought his burning hands to his mouth, blowing on

186

them and waving them in the air.

Just then, Norman's monitors and computers came to life. Lights started flashing, the computer instantly started checking Street Hawk for damage, and on the video monitor, Norman could see the same thing Jesse was seeing: Henri Dumos waving his hands frantically in the air, looking like some kind of idiot. Norman grinned; he was back in contact.

Jesse now heard for the first time over the roar of the fires the sound of police sirens. He looked toward the gate and saw that two police cars had already arrived, as well as the other members of the Protection Association. Phil's car still blocked the gate, but the fire was merely smouldering now, and several policemen were trying to squeeze past it.

'Jesse, the police!' Norman shouted. 'Get out of there!'

'Norman? We're a team again?' Jesse asked.

'Affirmative,' Norman said proudly. 'I have visual. Now get out of there.'

'One quick stop and I'm on my way.'

He powered Street Hawk forward, coming to a stop just in front of the trash dumpster. Phil and Joey stepped out of hiding.

'Don't be a local hero,' Jesse warned them. 'You can't take care of your family if somebody shoots you.'

The police were running toward him. Jesse shot forward and hit vertical lift, jumping the fence in one easy stroke.

'Nice jump,' Norman said excitedly. 'How does the bike feel?'

'It feels fine,' Jesse answered, 'but it wasn't the bike that was busted. How's it feel to you?'

Norman was as happy as a child on Christmas morning. 'It feels great, just great. Jesse, can I bring you in?'

'I'm in your hands.'

Norman quickly hit a series of switches on the console, moving his fingers with the assurance of a piano virtuoso. The computer instantly calibrated the most efficient route back to the Command Centre, and Norman started the countdown. The motorcycle launched into hyperthrust. Allowing himself the luxury of relaxation, Jesse let the computers and motorcycle do all the work for a change. He zipped through the streets at hundreds of miles per hour, too fast to even see the houses and the cars and the astonished looks on the faces of the people he flew past.

Jesse laughed.

When he got back to Command Centre, Jesse found Norman standing in front of the wall of whirring computer equipment with the biggest grin on his face he had ever seen. He waved expansively at the flashing row of lights and said, 'This is more like it, huh?'

'I'll say,' Jesse said, beaming despite himself.

'You up for a celebration?'

Jesse stared at him. This was totally unlike the Norman he was accustomed to. 'Are you serious?'

'Sure, I'm serious,' Norman said. 'You rounded up the gold robbers, right?'

Jesse nodded. 'Right.'

'And the computers are working again, right?'

Again, Jesse nodded.

Norman smiled warmly. 'And you proved the value of the human element over machines.'

Jesse looked at him. The smile on his face grew wider. He'd got through to Norman at last. 'Thank you, Norman.'

'No, it's the other way around,' Norman replied. 'Thank you, Jesse.'

Jesse nodded, and suddenly his eyes narrowed with suspicion. 'Does this mean I'm buying?'

Norman grinned. 'I certainly hope so.'

TWENTY-SEVEN

There was a huge flock of people crowded into Phil Simpkins' shop the following afternoon. Phil and Joey were in the centre of the room, relating for the third time that day their adventures of the night before. They included only minor deviations from the truth in their retelling, and their friends and neighbours regarded them with the kind of awe they usually reserved for football players and movie stars. Phil and Joey basked in all the attention.

'So then, while we were providing the diversion,' Phil said, 'Street Hawk shows up and he comes roaring down on these guys—'

The little bell above the door tinkled, and Phil stopped his story in mid-sentence as he saw Jesse enter the shop. 'Joey, you finish telling them,' he said. 'I want to talk to Jesse here.'

Phil pushed through the crowd of people pressed around him and met Jesse at the door. 'Let's go outside,' he whispered, and the two men stepped back out to the sidewalk.

'We did pretty good last night, huh Jesse?' Phil boasted.

'Yeah,' Jesse answered, looking through the window at the group of eager listeners gathered inside. 'But we don't want any press conferences.'

Phil jerked his thumb at the window. 'That stuff? Aw, don't worry about that. It's nothing. I promised you I

189

wouldn't talk to the press, and I mean it. I ain't a liar.' His voice softened, and he added quietly, 'I ain't a hero, either. I wanted to talk to you about what you said before, about how my organization could help the police force.'

'Wait a second, Phil,' Jesse said, holding up his hand. 'I'm still letting that business about not being a hero sink in.'

'It's true,' Phil admitted. 'It's just like you said. We can't handle everything ourselves; sometimes you gotta count on the police. Those guys last night, they were way out of our league. They would have killed us without a second thought. If Street Hawk hadn't shown up when he did, I wouldn't even be here today. And you know, I can't do my family any good if some guy shoots me. So the way I look at it, I'm going to let the cops take all the risks from now on. They know what they're doing. I just wanna do my best to help them out.'

'Does that go for Street Hawk, too?' Jesse said, goading him on just to hear his reaction.

'Hey, I don't know,' Phil said, not even sure what he meant at first.

'He's your guy, isn't he?'

Phil blushed. 'Listen, Jesse, you know you can't believe everything you read in the papers.'

'You can if you give them the story. You told them that Street Hawk was one of your boys,' Jesse reminded him.

'Well, not exactly—'

'Yes, exactly,' Jesse insisted. 'And the police force doesn't like him riding the streets like some sort of vigilante cowboy. If he's interested in fighting crime, he can join the Neighbourhood Watch Programme, just like you're doing, right? So you tell him that the next time you talk to him.'

'But I don't even know him!' Phil cried.

Jesse smiled. 'Maybe not. But he knows you.'

Phil gave him a funny look and Jesse patted him on the back. 'I've got to go, Phil. But come by the station on Monday, and we'll have a talk, okay?'

Leaving the confused plumber standing on the sidewalk, Jesse jumped into his Mustang and drove off. He glanced at his watch. It was just after five o'clock; Deborah would be finished shooting the spot pretty soon.

They were shooting over at Artie's studio. Several equipment trucks were parked on the street in front of the brownstone, but Jesse had no trouble finding an empty space. On his way up the stairs, he could hear the sound of a bittersweet piano solo emanating from the third floor loft, and he recognized the style instantly as that of Artie Shank. Reaching the landing, he quietly slid open the door and tiptoed inside. The shoot was in progress and, not wanting to disturb anybody, Jesse ducked behind a row of bright spotlights to watch.

Deborah was leaning on the piano, watching Artie move his ancient fingers across the ivories with the skill and assurance his years of experience had taught him. A microphone hung above their heads, and a camera was pointing at them. Rachel Adams and the director sat beside the camera, watching the performance with studied interest.

Artie's solo came to a melodious close and the final, sustained note hung in the air. Deborah smiled at him, saying, 'Thank you, Artie.' She turned to the camera. 'Remember, Artie Shank and I wouldn't kid you. There are people out there who do care. And they know, like Artie and I, that drugs are for dummies.'

She held her smile for a moment, and then the director shouted, 'Cut it! That's a wrap!' The director stood up. 'That was wonderful, you two. Just great.'

Rachel said, 'I agree. It was fabulous.'

She moved forward and shook Deborah and Artie's hands. Jesse watched from the back for a minute, and then he stepped out from behind the lights and approached Deborah.

A big smile appeared on her face as soon as Deborah saw him. She rushed forward and threw her arms around Jesse, startling him with a very ardent kiss. She moved away, and Jesse looked a bit embarrassed. 'Hi,' she said, eagerly.

'Hi, yourself,' he whispered. He looked up and saw Rachel gazing at him with a smirk on her face.

'Hello, Jesse,' she said, trying her best to restrain a giggle.

Jesse smiled shyly. He looked at Artie, who gave him a wink of encouragement. 'Let's get out of here,' he said to Deborah.

'Sure. See you, everybody,' she yelled, as she grabbed her purse. They headed out of the door, Jesse certain they'd be talking about them as soon as they were gone. Already, his ears were burning.

'What did you have in mind?' Deborah asked as they stepped outside.

'Oh, I picked up a couple steaks this morning,' Jesse replied. 'I thought we could barbecue them, have some wine—'

Jesse's beeper went off. His face fell. Norman wanted him to call in.

'What's that?' Deborah asked.

Jesse pulled out his beeper and looked at it. 'Oh, it's this darned beeper,' he said. 'It's busted again.'

'Are you sure? Because if it's something important—'

'No, no,' Jesse assured her. 'It's just busted.' He opened up the car door for her and Deborah climbed inside. 'I'm going to have to get a new one.'

Jesse threw the beeper into a nearby garbage can. He knew Norman would kill him for that, but the last thing he wanted on his mind tonight was Street Hawk. He climbed in behind the wheel and started the ignition.

'What are you humming?' Deborah asked.

'Huh?' Jesse hadn't even realized he had been humming. 'Oh, that's your song, "Golden Eyes". For some reason, I can't get it out of my head.'

He put the car in gear and they started for home. Deborah nestled up against him and Jesse put his arm around her, a contented smile on his face. On the street behind them, the trash can continued to beep insistently.